I0741605

WHAT IT MEANS

Myth, Symbol, and Archetype in the Third Millennium, Vol. 1

Eva Rome

also by Eva Rome

Travel for STOICs: Empowering the Solo Traveler Who Is Obsessive, Introverted, and Compulsive

Blue Morpho Press New Mexico
3201 Zafarano Dr., Suite C #218
Santa Fe, New Mexico 87507-2672 U.S.A.
www.bluemorphopress.net

Library of Congress Cataloging-in-Publication Data

Name: Rome, Eva, 1952– author.
Title: What It Means: Myth, Symbol, and Archetype in the Third Millennium / Eva Rome.
Description: Santa Fe: Blue Morpho Press New Mexico, 2019.
Identifiers: ISBN-978-0-9678995-4-1 (paperback)
Library of Congress Control Number: 2019918662
Subjects: 1. Fiction. 2. Humor. 3. Semiotics. 4. Anthropology. 5. Philosophy. 6. Psychology. I. Title.

Printed in the United States of America

Cover, book design, and illustrations by Laurie McDonald
Photograph of Laurie McDonald by Paulina Gwaltney

dedicated to

Susan Matthews
who suggested I write this book

and
Geoffry Oshman
Jo-Ann Joseph

Contents

Introduction 1

My Visit to La Brea 9

Leisure 15

The Roller Coaster Ride as Aristotelian Narrative 17

Indoor Skydiving and Dreams of Flying 25

Guilting 31

Objects 35

The Eyelash Curler as Monument 37

Lawn Ornaments 41

The Wienermobile 49

Chariots of the Gods and Vanity License Plates 53

Fidget Spinners 59

Secular Rituals 65

Car Wash as Surrogate Purification Ritual 67

3-D Archery 71

The Rattlesnake Roundup 77

Power Symbols 83

The Eyebrow as Female Power Symbol 85

The Avatar 91

Keith Richards's Magic Stick 97

Technology 103

QR Codes 105

The Cloud as Sixth Ocean 109
Segway 115
Acoustic Weapons 119
Food 125
Pringles Potato Chips 127
Energy Drinks 131
Peanut Butter and Jelly 135
Acknowledgements 139
Notes 141
Images 145
About the Author 155

INTRODUCTION

What It Means (*WHIM*) is a collection of essays that examines how myth, symbol, and archetype manifest in everyday American life in the early third millennium. *WHIM* was written for readers interested in cultural studies, mythology, language, human behavior, philosophy, and anthropology, and is also intended to be a text for future readers curious about life back in the CE 2000s. *What It Means* is a time capsule in written form, and for those who enjoy burying objects for future discovery, instructions for preserving it appear at the end of the introduction.

From generation to generation, the world's myths, symbols, and archetypes express their timeless qualities in compelling and uniquely contemporary ways, and *What It Means* interprets and illuminates this phenomenon. *WHIM* emerged from three sources: a dream my friend of fifty-plus years, Susan Matthews, had in 2015, in which her kitchen appliances were covered with a pattern of photo-real peanut butter and jelly sandwiches set in shiny Formica; a story I wrote about a fictional trip to La Brea Tar Pits in Los Angeles as a twelve-year-old; and the mid-twentieth century French literary theorists engaged in the study of semiology (the uses and interpretations of signs and symbols) and hermeneutics (the study of written, verbal, and nonverbal communication).

In an email response to Susan's dream, I included an invented analysis of the symbolism of peanut butter and jelly allegedly excerpted from *The Book of Symbols: Reflections on Archetypal Images* (Taschen Press, 2010). This short essay is the last entry in *What It Means*. When I confessed to the ruse, she suggested I write a book of parody essays in the pseudo-academic style of "Peanut Butter and Jelly," and *WHIM* is the result. But not all of the essays are pure parody; some include whimsical content, and some are a blend of fact and fiction. Some emulate the magical thinking—preposterous inferences based on speculation and personal bias—that appears occasionally in anthropological scholarship. I hope you can discern the differences.

In both a psychological and a semiological sense, at La Brea Tar Pits, where natural asphalt has formed pools of tar for tens of thousands of years, more is going on than what meets the eye. The centerpiece is a fabricated mastodon grouping—a father, a mother, and a baby—in the midst of a family crisis for which there is no possibility of redemption.

The father mastodon has unwittingly wandered into the main pit and become stuck in tar, and, wisely, the mother and baby have not followed suit. The father realizes his predicament and lifts his massive head to the heavens in supplication, while the baby extends its pitifully short trunk in the direction of his father, hoping to rescue him, suggesting a human child's hero fantasy: an opportunity to redeem himself for being inferior to the father in size, strength, age, and power. Because being stuck in tar can mean annihilation, it's a powerful metaphor, and worldwide, over two hundred and fifty stories on this theme have been documented, many of them replicating the narrative of our own Tar-Baby story of the Southern United States. All have to do with ensnarement with the threat of death. But unlike the clever rabbit—the hero of many of these ensnarement stories—the father mastodon has no hope of escape, creating a complicated and tragic meaning for his family. Tar is a black, sticky, mysterious, ominous goo that emits methane; and a pool of tar can be compared to what Carl Jung described as the shadow side of the personality: the irrational, unknowable dark side, the parts of us that we do not bring into consciousness. The scene of utter despair is a symbol of more than just a mastodon stuck in tar; it is a signifier of the failure and collapse of the family unit caused by a father inextricably mired in his shadow side, beyond hope of rescue or resurrection.

These deeper meanings that emerge at La Brea link to French semiological thought in general and to Roland

Barthes in particular. Barthes famously analyzed popular post–World War II consumer and entertainment culture, and *What It Means* aspires to be the early third millennium's answer to his insightful and funny work *Mythologies*. Published in 1957, *Mythologies* is a collection of essays that examines the bourgeois norm, as he puts it, and the appropriation-cum-transformation of myth to express modern meanings. *Mythologies* includes essays on "The Romans in Films" (why do Romans always have fringe bangs and sweaty bodies?), "Soap Powders and Detergents" (substances that vanquish evil and dirt and maintain the public order), and "Operation Margarine" (by examining the margarine versus butter dispute, Barthes illuminates the ways in which the establishment rids us of our prejudices). With Barthes as inspiration, *WHIM* is a survey of today's bourgeois norm in a collection of twenty-one short essays.

From the semiological point of view, Barthes approaches his subjects as studies of ideas manifest in form.

> The development of publicity, of a national press, of radio, of illustrated news, not to speak of the survival of a myriad rites of communication which rule social appearances makes the development of a semiological science more urgent than ever. In a single day, how many really non-signifying fields do we cross? Very few, sometimes none. Here I am, before the sea; it is true that it bears no message. But on the beach, what

> material for semiology! Flags, slogans, signals, signboards, clothes, suntan even, which are so many messages to me.[1]

Had Barthes lived to see the flourishing of television and the emergence of the internet, Instagram, Twitter, selfies, 3-D printing, virtual reality, and on and on, he would be overwhelmed by the sheer volume of material for his studies. Questing for those naturalized expressions of myth in popular culture, he'd never have to leave his desk.

The word "mythology" comes from the Ancient Greek *mythos*, meaning "report, tale, story," and *logos*, meaning "word" or "speech," so mythology is the written or spoken story of a people, expressing their beliefs and values in symbolic form. Myths attempt to answer the big questions of life: our human origins, the nature of good and evil, the meaning of suffering, the question of an afterlife. To help us understand myth, scholar of comparative mythology and religion Joseph Campbell spent his career asking *the* salient questions relating to myth: "What is the secret of timeless vision? From what profundity of the mind does it derive? Why is mythology everywhere the same, beneath its varieties of costume? And what does it teach?"[2] In no way am I equipped to answer those questions with the same erudition and finesse as either Campbell or Barthes, but I can point to leisure, objects, rituals, power symbols, technologies, and even foods of the third millennium that express these ideas.

Campbell also wrote,

> Throughout the inhabited world, in all times and under every circumstance, the myths of man have flourished; and they have been the living inspiration of whatever else may have appeared out of the activities of the human body and mind. It would not be too much to say that myth is the secret opening through which the inexhaustible energies of the cosmos pour into human cultural manifestation. Religions, philosophies, arts, the social forms of primitive and historic man, prime discoveries in science and technology, the very dreams that blister sleep, boil up from the basic, magic ring of myth."[3]

It is my hope that *What It Means* helps illuminate the mysteries that make us human, leading the reader through those secret openings that connect us to each other from age to age.

An archetype can be simply "a statement, pattern of behavior, or prototype which other statements, patterns of behavior, and objects copy or emulate."[4] The origin of the idea of archetypes is commonly attributed to Plato, and in more contemporary times, Carl Jung introduced the idea of the collective unconscious with its population of archetypes. Jung defined twelve primary archetypes that describe human motivations—among them the mother, the hero, the wise old man, the rebel, animals, even colors and shapes—but he also wrote that there is no fixed number of archetypes. Perhaps their numbers are *unlimited* and archetypes ageless. Archetypes have helped define the human psyche at least since proto-humans began expressing themselves on the walls of caves (and probably long before that), and *What It Means* links us to these ancient times, suggesting that we're not so different from Neanderthals after all.

As mentioned near the beginning of the introduction, *WHIM*'s compilation of essays is a time capsule text intended for future readers, and you may have purchased the book along with an aLOKSAK element-proof, military-grade protective bag. After reading *WHIM*, please place the book in its protective bag and consider burying it in a location meaningful to you. If you're remodeling your house or place of business, install *WHIM* in a wall, under some floorboards, or in the ceiling. Bury it in your backyard or along a favorite hike. And even though the aLOKSAK is waterproof to two hundred feet, please resist the temptation to consign *WHIM* to a body of water. If your copy of the book did not come with a bag, for a small fee you can order one, including instructions for burying, on the *What It Means* website (www.whatitmeansthebook.com). Since time capsules tend to get lost, I ask that you provide GPS coordinates of the book's interment site so that a record may be kept of all of *WHIM*'s time capsule locations. Please send these coordinates to bluemorphopress.nm@gmail.com.

At its most basic, *What It Means* is my interpretation of myths, symbols, and archetypes that have meaning for today and hopefully for *What It Means*'s readers. Decoding the strangeness of our contemporary world can be challenging, and *WHIM* provides (at least a few of) the answers to our sometimes-confusing, sometimes-chaotic existence. It is hoped that readers from the end of the twenty-first century and beyond will look back on *What It Means* to gain insights into, what will likely seem to them, the peculiarities of an earlier time.

My Visit to La Brea

From the moment I opened my elementary school science book and saw that picture, I was stuck on the idea. An artist's rendering of a noble mastodon trapped in tar made me obsess about making a pilgrimage to La Brea Tar Pits. The idea that this little repository of fossil wealth held objects up to forty thousand years old, including the bodies of over two thousand saber-toothed cats alone, took hold of my imagination like nothing else. I thought of the mystery of the Tar-Baby. In the story, you never really know where Brea Fox gets the tar to make his lure, but I'd assumed that the briar patch was just off the road to the Tar Pits. Then at some point it occurred to me that in the movie *Song of the South* I had misunderstood Uncle Remus's Southern accent. He was saying "Br'er" (brother) Fox and "Br'er" Rabbit—not "Brea."

For months, I carried my science book with me everywhere, and whenever I needed a little jolt of excitement, I'd open it up to the Tar Pits page. Once while I was running to my mom's car after school, I accidentally dropped the book on some freshly laid asphalt. Pages from the unit on spiders and flies landed face-down on the asphalt, so I didn't mind having to leave them behind. My book permanently acquired the olfactory ambience of tar. One day in Spanish class, I learned that a word for "the" is "la" and that "brea" means "tar," so I stopped referring to the Pits as The La Brea Tar Pits. It was like saying "The The Tar Tar Pits," and it made me feel smarter to know that.

I finally realized my dream when I was twelve. On a road trip from Fort Worth, Texas, to California with my family, I was perusing a travel guide in the back seat when I came across the same picture that was in my science book. The picture was captioned, "La Brea, downtown Los Angeles," our destination. But what were these photos of twenty-first century civilization doing next to it? The picture in my science book never suggested that the freeways, billboards, car dealerships, fancy hotels with big swimming pools, and gentlemen's clubs of Los Angeles may exist just outside the frame. Since the Pleistocene era was long past, I didn't really expect to see hirsute men clad in animal skins running down Wilshire Boulevard with clubs and spears chasing saber-toothed tigers. But the idea that the Pits could be surrounded by roofing companies and pothole repair trucks made me anxious. It was all because of our disappointing trip to the Alamo the summer before. Our school history books had depicted the Alamo as a single, majestic building visually disrupting the expanse of open plain in 1830s Texas. But today, it's right in the middle of downtown San Antonio, dwarfed by high-rise hotels and mid-century office buildings and overrun with guys dressed as Santa Anna's soldiers selling "Remember the Alamo" T-shirts and Davy Crockett coonskin caps. That's where I learned to be suspicious of what's lurking beyond the frame of a photograph or a drawing.

The sign for the Tar Pits came into view, and my heart began to race. Dad parked the car. We bounded up the steps two at a time to the observation deck and ran to the railing.

There, in a huge and deceptively watery tar pit, was the replica of the giant mastodon, hopelessly trapped and struggling in black goo, his massive trunk and tusks thrust into the air: a scene imagined by a great tragedian. That wild-eyed look animals get when they know they're done for conveyed the hopelessness of the situation. His mate stood stiffly and safely on the bank, not three feet away, while their child extended his pathetically short trunk, trying to touch Dad's flank. It was poignant. I bit my lip so I wouldn't burst into tears.

I started to think about all the creatures that had been trapped in the Tar Pits. Birds and lizards, glued like bugs on flypaper. A Bambie-like fawn innocently coming to the water's edge for a drink and sliding in, her spotted body struggling as all four legs, stiff as boards, slowly sank into the tar. Hungry carnivores cruising by and, in the process of making dinner out of Bambie, getting stuck themselves. Vultures, in a frenzy over all the carnage, circling in downdrafts and swooping into the Pits, the tar grabbing their wing tips and stopping their momentum dead. Nature is a murdering bitch, as the saying goes, and the Tar Pits were a blunt reminder of the cruelty and absurdity of life. Why had I never thought about the monstrous amount of suffering they had caused? And why were they one of L.A.'s biggest tourist destinations? I thought that said a lot about the human race. There I was, staring into the tarry abyss, measuring the depth of my own soul and the souls of the other tourists. What I saw was opaque, ominous, savage, black.

For weeks before my trip, I contemplated what I might like to throw into the pit to be preserved for all eternity and placed a few carefully curated objects into my backpack. I knew my mother wouldn't allow it, using the "if everyone threw something into the pit" argument I'd heard plenty of times before but in different contexts. But everyone *had* thrown something in. Styrofoam cups and soda cans, programs from the art museum next door, candy wrappers, pennies, shoes. Suddenly I knew exactly what it had to be: the wad of pink bubble gum lodged in my cheek. Like tar's cute cousin—a frivolous, sweet substance that posed no danger of extracting a tooth or cementing one's jaw closed—the gum signified both innocence and immortality, its bright pinkness a symbol of life and hope. When my mother wasn't looking, I blew a bubble and tossed it in, its landing making a muffled "plop," its buoyancy defiant of the death trap in which it floated.

What redeems this place of sorrow is an excellent exhibit inside the Page Museum (the institution that houses the bones of over two hundred species of animals extracted from the Pits) entitled "What It's Like to Be Stuck in Tar." The exhibit is basically a huge, circular vat partitioned into four sections. Liquid tar fills each section, and two metal rods per section protrude from the tar: a large rod for strong visitors and a smaller one that offers less resistance for weaker

Tar Pits patrons. You just stand there and try to pull the rods out of the tar, and no one had succeeded, not yet. This is how I know. A placard next to the vat misquotes the Father of our National Parks, John Muir, as saying, "When one tugs at a single thing in nature, he finds it attached to the rest of the world." (What he really said was "When we try to pick out anything by itself, we find it hitched to everything else in the Universe," but it's close enough.) If someone managed to dislodge a rod, I pictured this modest vat of tar sucking the entire contents of the world up into its bowl. Obviously no powerlifters or World's Strongest Man contestants know about the exhibit.

Later, in the gift shop, I discovered an old postcard from the '70s that featured a large group of kids surrounding the vat, experiencing what it's like to be stuck in tar and smiling about it. Had the scene outside of utter agony and defeat escaped their notice?

LEISURE

The Roller Coaster Ride as Aristotelian Narrative

Indoor Skydiving and Dreams of Flying

Guilting

The Roller Coaster Ride as Aristotelian Narrative

In his work *Poetics*, Greek philosopher Aristotle introduced the idea that a dramatic story should express a whole action comprised of a beginning, a middle, and an end. A protagonist—the hero—carries the action to completion, journeying through an emotional and psychological landscape that builds throughout the narrative and transforms the hero in a way of significance. Aristotle also believed a dramatic story is built on a single, story-catalyzing event. In the outer space film *Ad Astra,** astronaut Major Roy McBride undertakes a perilous journey to Neptune to search for a father who abandoned him light years ago. The catalyzing event? Intergalactic pulses that threaten Earth, sent by guess who. *Booksmart*'s* two brainy protagonists reach the end of high school and realize they don't know how to party. And Lynne Cheney's character in *Vice,** a film about her husband Dick's rise to political power, delivers the catalyzing event when she tells Dick—in no uncertain terms—that he'd better clean up his act or else. These single actions create stories made of two fundamental parts: complication (rising action to a climax) and unraveling (dénouement; literally, the action of untying). Exactly the point, according to Aristotle: The purpose of storytelling is to bring an audience to catharsis—literally a purification or cleansing—and to return the audience to a state of dramatic equanimity. When watching a film that follows the rules of Aristotelian structure, the viewer feels emotional ups and downs, the defeats and triumphs of the protagonist, the twists and turns of plot that threaten to derail the protagonist's quest, and the moment when all is lost, triggering the fear that the hero will fail to complete the journey dictated by the action. Like the Aristotelian narrative, a roller coaster ride is a plotting of the emotional imperatives of the dramatic story, and this creates its appeal.

The person who boards an indoor roller coaster ride at a theme park—The Revenge of the Mummy attraction at Universal Studios Hollywood is our example—embarks on the hero's journey in abbreviated form.

The Hero's Journey

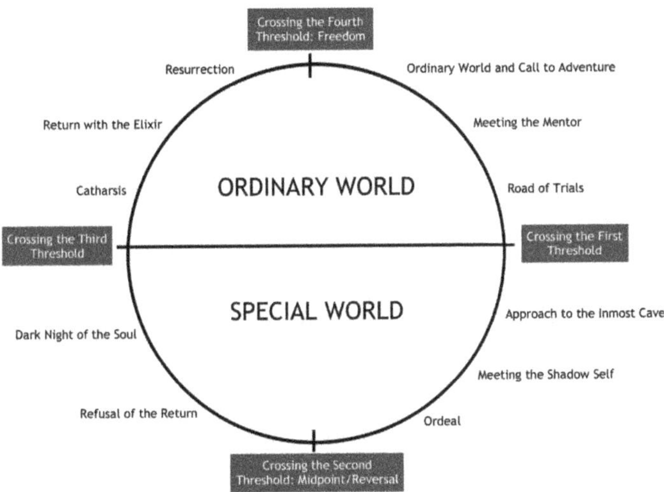

First, he receives a "call to action" delivered by various means—smartphone and television advertisements are the norm—challenging potential riders to embrace the experience, survive it, and achieve hero-status. Thus burdened by these provocations, he seeks the theme park, a departure from the ordinary world and an entry into a special world: an alternate reality or unfamiliar territory, the successful navigation of which is the primary challenge. By means of guidance provided in map form, the hero arrives at a long line of other adventure seekers assembled in a labyrinthine absurdity of stanchions and ropes designed to challenge everyone's patience. At a key moment, the hero arrives at a ticket booth, a contemporary Temple of Apollo where an emotionless Oracle of Delphi surrogate seals the hero's fate. The Oracle points to a digital display that gives the hero, ticket in hand, a glimpse into his future. The display warns, "This is a high-speed roller coaster ride that includes sudden and *dramatic* [italics mine] acceleration, climbing, tilting, dropping, and backwards motion." A deep, resonant voice, sounding as if it were transmitting live from the mummy's cavernous tomb, and conjuring drama out of what is essentially health and safety information, intones, "In order to experience Revenge of the Mummy, if you have heart, back, or neck issues, seizures, dizziness, claustrophobia, or any other conditions that may be aggravated by the experience, *turn back immediately* or suffer the consequences!" These messages both strengthen the hero's resolve and intensify the fear response. While shuffling along in line, restless with excitement, his emotions are manipulated by music alternating between ominous and upbeat, creating the emotional ups and downs that presage the experience to come.

After what seems like an interminable wait, the hero crosses the threshold and enters an ersatz Egyptian tomb: a narrow, twisting, sinister passage lit in nausea-inducing green light and decorated with mysterious carvings: scarab beetles flanked by vulture wings, jackal-headed human figures, and other harbingers of the chaos to follow. Wall niches house animatronic skeletons and mummies that attempt to grab him as he passes. To heighten the hero's sense of doom, a voice warns, "Run for your lives. The curse is real!" Chest-pounding, low-frequency sound effects and the descending pitch known as the "booj," commonly heard in movie trailers of the disaster genre, challenge the hero's ability to control his bowels.[1] Just as the claustrophobia and sonic assaults become nearly unbearable, he arrives at an ascending staircase that leads to a chain of mine cars: a conveyance that, like death, is inescapable once it has you in its grips. The hero is strapped in, warned to keep his head, hands, and feet inside the car; and if an accomplice is too portly, or frail of heart or mind, he is not allowed to board at all. A safety rail locks in place. The operator of this multicar transport, the "mentor," reiterates the set of rules, designed not only to prevent accidents but also to create anticipation of the frenzied ride ahead, triggering the fight, flight, or freeze response in advance of the actual experience. The mentor flips a switch, amygdalas are on high alert, and the journey to catharsis begins.

The instant the roller coaster cars begin to move, the "ordeal" and the "refusal of the return" in the narrative is reached. The line of cars creeps into a tunnel of doom, populated with cutlass-wielding warrior mummies who scream and moan and slash at our hero. The huge, partially decomposed head of Imhotep, an Egyptian polymath from the twenty-seventh century BCE and the antagonist of the *Mummy* movies, appears and declares "Serve me and savor the riches of eternal life!" As our hero plunges at high speed into total darkness, twisting and turning, his body in a terrifying free fall, Imhotep declares “Now your souls belong to me!” He is subjected to swarms of scarab beetles, clouds of steam, and a trial by fire, and slams to a stop before smashing into a wall. But all is not lost: He eludes Imhotep’s final grasp, and with a protracted “NOOOOO,” Imhotep’s spell is broken. Catharsis is reached.

Our hero emerges from the tomb—dramatic action completed—and buys an “I Survived The Revenge of the Mummy” T-shirt, a symbol of power and fortitude and a sign of his heroism. This appropriation and conveyance of an object—the “return with the elixir”—from the special world to the ordinary world is essential to the resolution of the Aristotelian narrative, signifying a successful hero’s journey in a single, wearable, nonshrinking, 100% cotton image.

* All films released in 2019.

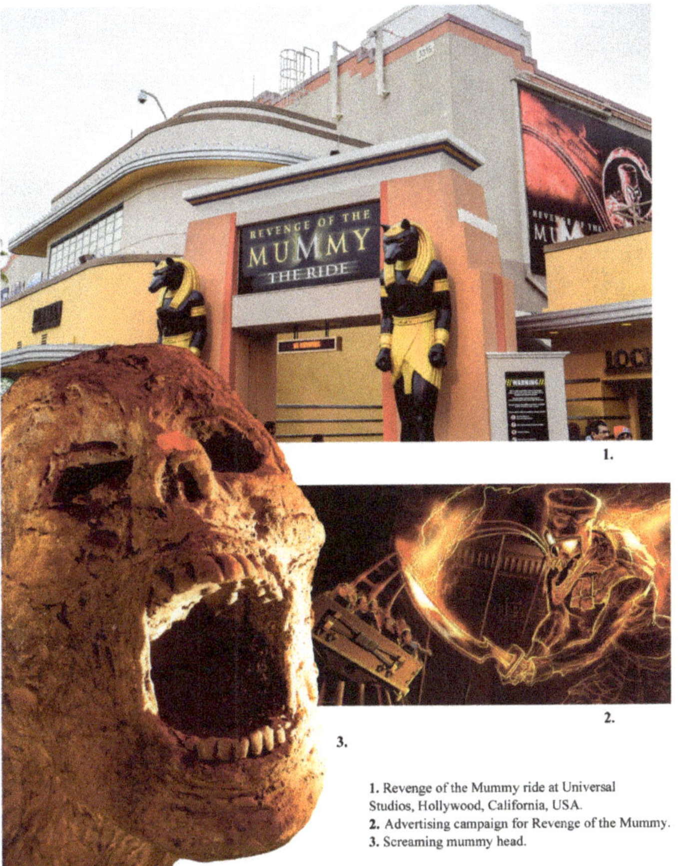

1. Revenge of the Mummy ride at Universal Studios, Hollywood, California, USA.
2. Advertising campaign for Revenge of the Mummy.
3. Screaming mummy head.

Indoor Skydiving and Dreams of Flying

In actuality a misnomer, indoor skydiving is not about simulating the experience of jumping out of an airplane at thirteen thousand feet; it's about being held aloft by a hurricane-force column of air that travels through a cylindrical tube, bottom to top. With indoor skydiving, the participant feels no accompanying vertigo, stomach and bowel distress, or intense fear that the novice jumper experiences on a virgin dive from an airplane, and the ground is never more than a few feet away. So what is the appeal of this third millennium leisure activity? It's the waking-life experience of the flying dream and is replete with psychological meanings.

Consider the myth of Daedalus and Icarus, the flying father-and-son duo who could have benefited from the more trustworthy avian-inspired technologies of our time. Daedalus, whose name means "cunningly wrought," was a talented inventor and the designer of the famous Labyrinth of Crete—built to imprison the ferocious Minotaur—but Daedalus angered his patron, King Minos, and he and his son Icarus were themselves banished to the Labyrinth to be tormented by the savage half-man, half-bull creature.[1] Being a clever inventor, Daedalus made a pair of wings for himself and for Icarus, covering them in a coating of wax, in order to escape the Labyrinth by air. Daedalus instructed Icarus not to fly too close to the sun, but, as children will do, he ignored his father. The heat softened the wax, and Icarus plunged to his death in the sea. What Daedalus and Icarus could have used was a powerful column of air that would whisk them away to safer territory.

Throughout recorded history, human beings have expressed the desire to fly. Fossil remains of proto-humans found on Norway's Engel Island, primarily at the base of a particularly steep cliff, tell a curious story: Male skeletons have wing-like appendages attached at the shoulder with rope made of animal sinew. Forensic archaeologists have observed multiple traumatic injuries to these skeletons, such as fractured bones and crushed skulls, the combined data suggesting early attempts at flight. Carbon dating of the remains suggests these were young men, not older than eighteen to twenty years of age, who possibly died during an initiation ritual or in an adolescent act of hubris.

1.

2.

1. Bodyflyer in a FlyStation facility, St. Petersburg, Russia.

2. Herbert James Draper, *The Lament for Icarus*, 1898.

Fast forward several thousand years to the fifteenth century, and Leonardo da Vinci has strapped himself to a flying machine of his invention. That attempt did not end well, either, but thankfully Leonardo survived the experiment.

The urge to fly signifies a longing for the transcendent, a desire to mingle with the celestial (or to be a celestial), and this wish has been subconsciously coded into a language that manifests in our repertoire of dream scenarios. Dream researchers worldwide have concluded that the flying dream is the fifth most common dream of all peoples, with falling through a volume of space, being chased, losing teeth, and showing up at an important event missing a critical article of clothing occurring more commonly than the flying dream. There are as many interpretations of the flying dream as there are dreamers: Koreans believe a flying dream indicates an imminent rise of status or the success of a relationship; in Islam, a flying dream means the fulfillment of aspirations; and the Chichumanga of Ecuador believe a flying dream is an actual out-of-body experience. Dreams often communicate their meanings via the literal; e.g., when the dreamer is flying, he or she may have “risen above” something: both escaping the Earth plane and perhaps responsibilities also, while avoiding everyday obstacles that cross his or her path. The dreamer may have a “flight of the imagination;” the dreamer may enter a lucid dream state where flying can be controlled.

As is to be expected, Sigmund Freud and Carl Jung had plenty to say about the flying dream as expressions of the psyche. Worth quoting is this passage from Freud:

> The extraordinary characteristic of the member of being able to raise itself against the force of gravity, one of the phenomena of erection, leads to symbolic representations by balloons, aeroplanes, and more recently, Zeppelins. The dream has another far more expressive way of symbolizing erection. It makes the sex organ the essential part of the whole person and pictures the person himself as flying. Do not feel disturbed because the dreams of flying, often so beautiful, and which we all have had, must be interpreted as dreams of general sexual excitement, as erection dreams.[2]

So raising oneself up against the force of gravity, the action of the erection, may be the salient appeal of indoor skydiving. The cylindrical column of air itself is a signifier of a powerful erection, and the human body, customarily seen in a vertical position, becomes a horizontal suspension in the wind tunnel, a phallus independent of its owner. Those who avail themselves of indoor skydiving facilities may suffer from a castration complex—women symbolically—and the act of being suspended in the horizontal position, by means of an invisible but powerful force, may restore confidence in both masculine and feminine sexual prowess. Dreams of flying, and realizing these dreams via indoor skydiving, are both expressions of the desire to fly free of fear and taboos. Thus, indoor skydiving is one of the most exhilarating and psychologically validating experiences available to the third millennium entertainment-seeker.

Guilting

According to the White Hutchinson Learning and Leisure Group, "a September 2013 Harris Interactive poll asked 2,577 American adults, 'Thinking of the time when you are not working or in school, what would you say your two or three favorite leisure time activities are?'" The report concluded that the favorite leisure activities of 2% of Millennials (age 18-36) and 3% of Gen-Xers (age 37-48) is "sewing, needle work, and guilting [sic]."[1] Granted, these age groups engage in other leisure activities far more often than in guilting; regardless, guilting deserves examination and analysis.

Guilting is the deliberate, and sometimes malicious, ensnaring of a person in an argumentative interaction with the intent of shaming him or her into apologizing. Commonly known as the "guilt trip," guilting involves a premeditated set of questions or statements designed to force a person to admit to behavior in which they may or may not have engaged. The accuser may extract a confession, or, more satisfyingly, catch his or her target in a lie. Integral to guilting is behaving as if you are a victim, when you are, in actuality, victimizing the other person. For example, the accuser may say to his or her partner, "You've been out drinking with my best friend. How can you do this to me? After everything I've done for you!" To which the accused will reply with either the truth, a lie, an equivocation, a placation, an apology, or any number of reactions. The salient point is that guilting has produced the desired effect: guilt, and the continuation, if not the strengthening, of the power structure of the relationship.

Technologies of the third millennium have both refined and expanded the delivery system of guilting. One need not be in the presence of another person for guilting to occur; a mere emoji (a tiny icon used to express an emotion or to represent an object) can communicate resentments or disapproval via any digital device, as can texting words to your target such as "sel" combined with the emoji for "fish," or neologisms such as "pissappointed," "torqued," or "agro." Using expressions like "Don't U want me to be (insert happy emoji here)?", "Why RU always at the gym and never with me?", or "Don't be so (an emoji for a negative trait or behavior)" are but a few examples of effective strategies to employ while spending leisure time guilting.

OBJECTS

The Eyelash Curler as Monument

Lawn Ornaments

The Wienermobile

Chariots of the Gods and Vanity License Plates

Fidget Spinners

The Eyelash Curler as Monument

Among the tools found in archaeological trash piles known as middens, researchers have identified a curious arched bone tool, made from the topmost rib—the shortest and most curved—of a pygmy sloth-like creature. By testing for indentation-induced surface distortion, scholars determined that the tool appeared to be weakened over time from repeated heating. Corroborating this finding was its somewhat blackened appearance, perhaps from soot from a fire or from pigment transferred to the tool. Because the bone measured approximately three centimeters (1.2 inches) long, because of the degree of curve of the arch, and because the tool was found in the proximity of several small pots of color used for the purpose of bodily adornment, archaeologists believe the tool was an early eyelash curler.

Certain content identified in cave paintings also supports this notion. Our early ancestor-artists observed and recorded many examples of the arch occurring in nature, from the curve of the Milky Way and the planetary ecliptic, to the arch of the foot and the subtle arch of the upper eyelid, self-referentially painted on naturally arched rock formations, including the caves themselves in which they dwelled. What appear to be instructions for applying eye make-up are communicated pictorially in a series of panels resembling the modern-day graphic novel. Thus, the venerable practice of eyelash curling was born with proto-hominids.

Fast forward to the third millennium, and the eyelash curler of today has evolved into an object that exists not only to enhance the appearance of its user but also as an aesthetic object in itself. When offered for sale in a clear plastic rectangular prism, it suggests a precious museum object encased in bulletproof glass, protected from the elements and from the touch and breath of curious museum-goers. Often featuring a silver or gold finish, the modern eyelash curler signals expensive, and with the addition of ornamental bling—a term that arose at the fin de siècle of the second millennium, meaning the ostentatious display of wealth via jewelry—the eyelash curler is a sign of incalculable wealth.

Let's examine the eyelash curler as the technological marvel that it is. Its salient feature, of course, is the arch.

Everything about its design exists to support the arch and its function in compressing the user's eyelashes into a dramatic and alluring upturn. This is of interest because it's the *opposite* of the usual function of an arch in architecture. The arch supports weight, and so functions as a structural element in buildings: in vaulted ceilings and in blind arches (arches used as support but filled in with solid materials), in bridges, in triumphal arches, as flying buttresses, and in the human foot. The eyelash curler supports no load at all and, interestingly, is a catenary arch; i.e., a curve that is created under its own weight when secured only at its ends, like free-hanging power cables or a chain supported by stanchions. With the exception of the Gateway Arch in St. Louis, Missouri—also a catenary arch—we are hard-pressed to find examples of arch for arch's sake.

So the eyelash curler is an exaltation of the arch, an object that exists only for the utility of the arch and its compression function. Because the eyelash curler is the only example of a mechanical device that uses *two* arches in compression, thus creating an arch effect in its most elemental form (arches that coarctate but do not support weight), the author of this book would like to propose an architectural monument to the estimable eyelash curler. Installed in Milan, the fashion capital of the world, opposite the Arco della Pace (the Arch of Peace), the Monument to the Eyelash Curler, a blinged-out kinetic curler rotating on a circular pedestal, would open and close as if it were a perpetual motion machine, reminding motorists and pedestrians alike of the timeless form and function of this immortal object.

The Arco della Pace (the Arch of Peace) and the Monument to the Eyelash Curler, Milan, Italy.

Lawn Ornaments

A Virgin Mary statue in an upended bathtub-grotto, placed in a front yard, signals the presence of a Catholic family inside the home. But what do the varieties of other lawn ornaments that have proliferated during the third millennium signify? A plethora of subtle meanings are attached to lawn ornaments of all kinds. As one strolls or drives through a neighborhood, encountering plastic flamingos, gnomes, reflective balls, and metal mariachis displayed in front yards, one instinctively knows the philosophical outlook, the psychological health, and the political leanings of the people who ornament their yards. For example, a single plastic flamingo, standing on one leg in a dingy front yard pond, signals a person who is perhaps of late middle age, lives alone, and is probably suffering from a mild case of ablutophobia, or the irrational fear of bathing, washing, or cleaning. On the other hand, a whole lawnful of flamingos suggests something very different: This is the work of an extrovert with herding tendencies articulating the need to control and contain by creating a coral-colored condition of uniformity (think: "in the pink") for what may in fact be an otherwise chaotic life. The flamingo lawn may also suggest that the owner of the home wishes to be vacationing on a tropical beach, especially if this display is seen in a desert environ.

Gnomes are displayed by misanthropes masquerading as folksy, jokester types. Traditionally, gnomes are secretive chthonic spirits that can move through solid earth as we humans move through air, and when given the opportunity to interact with humans, gnomes will concoct all manner of mischief and mayhem. Some gnome owners mistakenly think of their cute little statues as guardian angels of sorts, or protector-gods, when in fact they are the antithesis of anything heavenly or Olympian. Like their unsettling relative, the Elf on a Shelf, gnomes allegedly come alive at night to prowl for sweets dropped on sidewalks and to swim in neighborhood pools. Gnomes are also thieves, believed to be hoarders of all kinds of loot in underground vaults. Gnome ornaments are often engaged in some kind of solitary and often passive-aggressive or overtly offending activity; e.g., pointing a gnome-sized rifle out to the street, reading a book while sitting on a toilet, flashing passersby, or giving them the finger. These gnomes have their special meanings, all signifying to the visitor to stay away: The owner is engaged in like activities in which you are not welcome to join (nor would you want to). So to display a gnome in one's yard sends a powerful message to potential interlopers: Be wary and approach at your own risk, keep a close watch on your valuables, and if you dare to stay, don't expect any measure of hospitality.

Reflective ball owners are unapologetic narcissists who live in the fantasy of their distorted, mirrored image and the image of their house and environs. These people spurn visitors, keep obsessively clean households, and tend to be emaciated because they forget to eat. If this describes a neighbor of yours, and the postman has delivered their mail to you by mistake, just leave it at their doorstep, ring the doorbell, and run. "Impromptu" is not in their vocabulary. Skip this house if you're selling door to door, singing Christmas carols, or sharing the teachings of Jehovah. If you're driving past this house, don't even slow down.

Instrument-playing frogs signal a friendly household. This ornament combines the symbolism of the frog with the emotional qualities that music embodies. We all know that the frog is a symbol of love—cf. the Frog Prince fairy tale where a kiss from a beautiful princess transforms a frog into a handsome prince—and one can easily imagine the frog band playing Ziggy Marley's song "Changes":

> Change for the better and not for the worse
> Let's stand together and break our curses.[1]

1. Metal lawn ornament musical frogs.
2. Exhibitionist garden gnome, Pirna, Germany.
3. Bathtub madonna, Somerville, Massachusetts, USA.

Consider a frog's life, which begins as a tiny, wiggly tadpole that absorbs its tail and transforms into an adult frog—an almost alchemical process—and the frog will possess seemingly magical powers. As recorded by Ovid, Classical mythology abounds with examples of these kinds of happy transformations. Of course, metamorphosis, according to Kafka, can also mean estrangement and alienation, but this meaning is absent here. More important, frogs inhabit two very different worlds, those of water and of land, moving seamlessly from one to the other, breathing (inspiring) with both gills and lungs, signified by the trumpet-playing member of the frog band. But frogs are also symbols of disgust, and the second plague of Egypt, as described in the Bible, consisted of a rain of frogs. Frogs have their own shadow, as we all do.

So what does this signify for the instrument-playing frog ornament owner? This is a warm, welcoming household that is never vexed by the unannounced drop-in. Many children in various stages of development live in this house, the frog being a powerful fertility symbol. Music is important to this household and is an activity that creates resilient bonds among its members. This home is replete with joy and exuberance. No cockroaches impinge on this home's hygiene.

Additionally, the lawn ornament can be a painful (symbolic) reminder of the universal experience of death and bereavement. An acquaintance reported the following relevant story.

My next-door neighbor, we'll call him Michael, had recently lost the last remaining member of his family and was very sad and lonely. I learned of his fondness for ducks as a child and decided that a plastic duck family that I'd seen at a local garden shop might cheer him up. I purchased the duck family, and on a Monday morning waited for Michael to go to work so I could install it in his front yard.

I planted the mother duck firmly into the turf by means of a tapered protrusion on the underside of her plump, vacuum-molded body. Three obedient baby ducks lined up behind her, looking up inquisitively as if waiting for instructions. When Michael came home from work and discovered the duck family, he seemed very taken—at first, anyway—with this addition to his perfectly manicured yard. But the ducks' bodies blocked the sunlight from reaching the St. Augustine grass immediately under them, so after a few days the grass began to turn brown and soggy with the frequent afternoon rains that were common for that time of year. So Michael was obliged to relocate the duck family every couple of days to another spot in the yard. For a while, he found it amusing to position them in different configurations—the mother duck following the babies, one of the ducklings lost in a far-flung part of the yard, the mother duck hiding from the babies in some bushes, etc. But Michael lost interest in his new family dangerously fast, and one day I saw them all lying on their sides in the barbecue pit. Michael claimed that he had innocently placed them there when the lawn needed mowing, and he forgot to reinstall them in the yard. It never occurred to him that from my viewpoint the scene looked morbid. But I accepted his explanation and replaced the duck family in the closely cropped yard with the babies in a semicircle around their mother.

Within a few more days, the ducks were scattered around the front porch and the mother's side had collapsed inward as if someone had stomped on her. When I confronted Michael about this, he said that high winds during the night had blown them around and this was how he'd found the mother in the morning. I returned the mother duck to her original shape and dispersed the family back into the yard, making sure they were secured deeply into the turf. The next day the ducks were missing from their places again. Following an extensive search, they turned up under some thick bushes, looking like they'd been dragged behind a car through muddy, rocky streets. Michael said a pack of dogs had squeezed through the backyard fence and assaulted the poor plastic creatures, shuttling them off into the bushes to bury them like bones…

For Michael, the ducks were indeed signifiers of his lost family. Buried deep in his subconscious, he had connected his early fondness for ducks with his departed relatives and was averse to the idea of being governed by the incorporeal. He had developed into a sufferer of one of the world's most obscure phobias: anatidaephobia. Anatidaephobia is the fear that at any time and in any place, a duck may be watching, and the thought of any member of the *Anatidae* family keeping tabs on his every action, as if it were his own family looking down on him from heaven, was intolerable for Michael. So as a signifier, the plastic duck family was a threat of great proportions.

Before placing lawn ornaments of any kind in one's yard, consider the deep significance and transferences that can occur, and make your selections carefully.

The Wienermobile

"All elongated objects," wrote Freud, "sticks, tree-trunks, and umbrellas (on account of the stretching-up which might be compared to an erection!) all elongated and sharp weapons, knives, daggers, and pikes, are intended to represent the male member."[1] A modern addition to that list: the Oscar Mayer Wienermobile.

A phallic symbol supreme, the Wienermobile is a portable, drivable emblem of the prepotent male culture: a reminder of male domination, power, and authority disguised as a larger-than-life-size child's toy. Shaped like a curved hot dog sitting on a bun and painted bright yellow and orange, the Wienermobile is covertly used to assert the male hegemony across America. Several sizes of Wienermobile—including one made from a Dodge RAM chassis, one from a

Willys Jeep, and another from a MINI Cooper—represent the range and variety of male genitalia.

The Oscar Mayer Wienermobile MINI Cooper, 2008

The Oscar Mayer Wienermobile , 1953

Visiting as many as four hundred cities per year, the Wienermobile subconsciously promotes promiscuous intercourse. Because the Wienermobile's wiener is semi-erect, when seen driven into a tunnel, the suggestion of vaginal penetration by a penis is indisputable.

As in our culture, where genitalia and human sexuality receive way more attention than the subject deserves, the Wienermobile continues a long line of phallic imagery that appears in all major world cultures: from the ancient Greeks east to India and Japan to the Toltecs, Mayans, and indigenous civilizations of South America. Phallic architecture was rampant in ancient Egypt, and Herodotus records in his *Histories* that the Athenians celebrated Priapus Day, where, during the weeks of preparation leading up to the festival, women spent day and night stuffing sheep entrails with ground meat and sacred herbs, presaging the modern hot dog. Before ingesting, a milky substance thickened with gluten and sweetened with honey was applied to the ancient hot dog, symbolizing ejaculate. This delicacy was enjoyed by all, and the celebration of Priapus Day, a favorite holiday of the ancient Greeks, soon spread along the rim of the Mediterranean.

As of this writing, eleven Wienermobiles travel the country, their drivers referred to as Hotdoggers. Hotdogger candidates are chosen from an elite group, all in their sexual prime, all college seniors about to graduate from Ivy League institutions. Wearing hot dog costumes, they pass out

Wienerwhistles to enthusiastic customers, the blowing of which is symbolic fellatio. Need I remind you that wiener is slang for "penis"?

The Wienermobile was first introduced in 1936, right on the heels of the Planters Nutmobile, a giant peanut on wheels, which came out just the year before. As described in the *What It Means* essay "Peanut Butter and Jelly,"

> Peanuts, a legume, develop their pods underground, and were first discovered and cultivated by the ancient Sumerians. Because of their scrotum-like structure and texture, and the fact that they usually contain two seeds, one per pod, they became a fertility symbol and were worshipped as such.

Seen driving down a highway in tandem, with the Wienermobile in the lead and the Nutmobile following, the message is clear. Could their respective manufacturers have possibly meant anything else?

Chariots of the Gods and Vanity License Plates

Perhaps more than any other industry professionals, car manufacturers understand what make consumers tick and play to those psychologies. Much has been studied and written about the automobile and its relationship to owner ego and the marking of territory that cars and driving represent. It is well-known that consumers are manipulated into buying vehicles that best express their identities and life-views and that communicate to other motorists—in an instant—who's behind the wheel. Clearly, a car is an extension of its owner's persona, and the driver assumes special (imagined) powers when he or she enters the vehicle and activates the car/driver relationship.

Let's examine a few offerings of the Ford Motor Company. When introduced in 1985, the Ford Taurus became immensely popular, and when production paused temporarily in 2007, seven-and-a-half million Tauruses had been built and driven. Was its appeal the unusual, futuristic form with its back window shaped like a television screen? Partially. The deeper meaning emerges from elsewhere: from a nuanced interdependence of the id (the instinctual) and the ego (the rational) that suspends the functioning of the superego (the conscience). To demonstrate this, let's examine the mythology of Taurus the bull.

Taurus was a huge, powerful, and destructive bull who terrified everyone he encountered. Wild and out of control, Taurus trampled everything in his path until he met Persephone, the Greek goddess of spring and renewal. Persephone was a calming presence, and only she could control Taurus, teaching him patience and how to use his strength in positive ways. People born under the Zodiac sign of Taurus thus are commonly thought of as stubborn but reliable, practical, good with finances, with a singular eye for beauty, and sensual. It is these characteristics that draw people to the Taurus automobile and that create the desire to own and drive one. The Taurus signifies these qualities, and other drivers instinctively know to keep a practical distance from this stampeding bull, while approving of the owner's choice of an aesthetic yet sensible automobile.

Another Ford product is the car named for the Greek god Orion, son of Poseidon and a mortal, a great hunter armed with an unbreakable club of solid bronze who, like Jesus of Nazareth, had the ability to walk on water. Possessed of an immense ego, Orion boasted that he could kill any beast on Earth, but was vanquished by the sting of a scorpion and placed among the stars by Artemis, the powerful huntress. Orion is perhaps the most recognizable constellation in the skies of North America, and Orion the car shares this recognizability with its namesake. Owners of Orion automobiles communicate to their fellow drivers this no-nonsense, get-out-of-my-way-I'm-behind-the-wheel quality, but there is a hidden, reckless vulnerability to these drivers, too.

Without a doubt, a richness of astrological signification is employed in the naming of vehicles. Other examples include: the Ford Galaxie; the Subaru (Japanese for the cluster of seven stars known as the Pleiades); the Chevrolet Nova, Vega, and Astro; the Saturn Sky; the Mitsubishi Eclipse; the Toyota Camry Solara; and the Mercury Comet (two celestial objects in one). Of all the chariots of the gods, the Eclipse is perhaps the most aptly named. Subconsciously feared when encountered on the road, the Eclipse induces a dread response in the limbic brains of other drivers, creating a direct link to ancient people's terror of the Earth being swallowed during a solar eclipse and all life perishing.

Thus, drivers who choose to own a celestial automobile communicate to the rest of us mortals that they see themselves as gods and goddesses and their conveyances divine. The implicit special powers of the immortals are conferred to the owner/driver and underpin this message of superiority. While traveling on the highway, best stay the recommended six car lengths behind these vehicles—more for those with vanity license plates.

One in ten license plates in Virginia, home to many of our politicians, is a vanity license plate, and in the whole of the United States, over nine million drivers choose to personalize their plates. What drives a person to acquire a vanity plate? Why are nine million of us willing to pay sometimes thousands of dollars, with one-off novelty plates costing millions, to define ourselves to our fellow drivers via a signifier of only seven letters and/or numbers, or fewer?

Archaeologists of the next millennium will surely be confused by the aluminum rectangles they find in the copious trash heap remains resulting from our third millennium excesses. What we call vanity plates will seem like obscure nonsense to those trying to parse their use and meaning. At first glance, they may be construed as some kind of ornament or large piece of jewelry worn around the neck, suspended from a chain or leather cord, identifying the wearer as a member of a mystery cult; e.g., EVILMOM and HOMICDL. Because of the obscurity of their messages, other vanity plates will be the subject of intense debate: OMGWTF, TRFYWIF, and MOFO are examples. Sexual references appear in abundance: LOVES69, 8EROUT, BLOWME, AVGPNIS, LKMYJNK. The more philosophically minded archaeologists will interpret the messages of these strange rectangles as pithy statements synthesized from the contemplation of existence: IAMLOST, RULOST, CRZYWMN, BGR8TFL, VANITAS, HWY2HEL. Some plates reference food and states of being: IH8PEAS, MEATBL, ILV2EAT, SPAM, DRUNK, TRIPPIN, CARSICK; hence, their meaning is less vague. Hopefully, someone will discover the self-referential plate that provides the salient clue to these objects' function during their time of use: LCNSPL8. Other vanity plates will merely be consigned to museums housing curious antiquities: FUN2BME, SRFBUM, JUSAYIN, DAMIML8, ALWYZL8, HIOFFCR, BYOFFCR, PMS24-7, IDIOT, NERD, DAMSTR8, GODDESS.

Vanity license plates link to a second century CE practice in Istanbul, then called Byzantium. Septimus Severus, a Roman emperor bent on conquering much of the Mediterranean world, was part of an equestrian family, and Septimus was responsible for building the Hippodrome in Byzantium, whose chariot races were the inspiration for the film *Ben Hur.* To distract his opponents, Septimus outfitted his chariots with the equivalent of vanity license plates. The "plate," forged of the highest-quality bronze, featured the engraved name of the charioteer and his preferred profanity, oaths, and expletives, with the intention of insulting and disarming his rivals. The more vulgar, the better. Examples of what became known as the *Profanus lamini* reside in a special adults-only section of the Topkapi Palace Museum in Istanbul.

Fidget Spinners

Fidget spinners are modeled after the triskelion, a sacred symbol originating during the Neolithic era—approximately 10,000 BCE through 2,000 BCE—based on three conjoined Archimedean spirals emanating from a center point. This powerful symbol appears in cultures throughout the world: stamped into Greek coins and painted on vases, stitched on coats-of-arms and on flags, carved into sacred stones, and incorporated into architectural designs. The number three itself has significance that repeats in many cultures, an obvious example being the Christian Bible's celebrated trio: the Father, the Son, and the Holy Ghost. A symbol of Tibetan Buddhism called the Gankyil, a triple spiral called the "wheel of joy," represents the triplicities found in Buddhism: the three wisdoms (learning, reflection, meditation); the three jewels (Buddha, Dharma, Sangha); and the three vajras (mind, speech, body).

In Hinduism, the Trimurti ("three forms" in Sanskrit) represents another triple deity: Brahma the creator, Vishnu the preserver, and Shiva the destroyer. In pagan cultures, the number three can mean body, mind, and spirit; past, present, and future; life, death, rebirth; creation, preservation, destruction; and on and on. When in motion, the fidget spinner's three whirling shapes appear to blend into a single circle, signifying the unity of the many into one and symbolizing the impermanence of a steady state of being. Thus, the fidget spinner represents the Chinese concept known as *Wújí*, the "one" from which everything is derived, the absolute underlying principle of the universe.

From the fidget spinner's Amazon description:

> Great Design For Anxiety, Focusing, ADD, ADHD, Autism, Quitting Bad Habits, Staying Awake On Long Car Drives, etc. Helps Relieve Stress. Perfect Size Suitable for Adults and Kids. Hold the spinner in one hand and use the other hand to spin it rapidly using small continuous strikes. With practice, spinners can be spun using one hand only, using the fingers of one hand to stop and start spinning. These are perfect pocket pieces for people wanting something small, simple, discrete and fun—it is also effective for focus, stress relief and deep thought.

1. 2.

1. Fidget spinner.
2. The triskelion.
3. Triskelion crop circle, England.
4. Buddhist Gankyil.
5. Three Legs of Man, national symbol of the Island of Man, U.K.
6. Church window triskel.

3.

4.

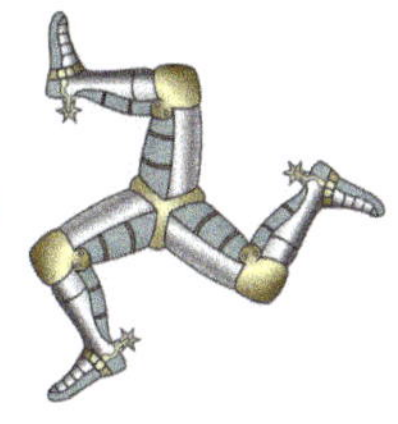

5.

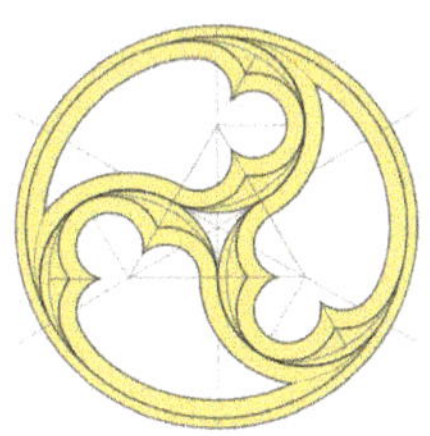

6.

Although it's doubtful that the next round of Nobel laureates will be thanking the fidget spinner for their work's inspiration, the spinner may have helped one or two of them quit biting their fingernails or clicking their retractable pens while deep in thought. But despite its name, the fidget spinner is much more than the third millennium's version of worry beads. Given the appearance of the triskelion design worldwide over thousands of years, even today appearing in mysterious vortices and crop circles theoretically hewn by aliens, the fidget spinner continues the long history of this important symbol. But the substance of the fidget spinner is more profound than meets the eye. Despite its common use as a mere toy, the fidget spinner is in actuality a gyroscope in miniature, producing its own vortex of whirling air when in motion. Like the famous butterfly effect of chaos theory, the combined disturbance of weather patterns created by the world's fidget spinners may be contributing to global warming.

Because of their round design, coins are easy to spin. Since the triskelion design appears on Greek, Celtic, English, Indian, and even Burundian coins, one wonders if perhaps ancient peoples used their coins for the purposes outlined by the Amazon seller. Did Lao Tzu, Confucius, Plato, and Herodotus all carry addictive fidget devices in their robes? Seneca himself writes that if not for the tactile stimulation provided by the first century CE's equivalent of the fidget spinner, a string of three triskelion-imprinted coins known as *nómisma klóstis*, he would never have had the focus to pen *On the Shortness of Life*.

SECULAR RITUALS

Car Wash as Surrogate Purification Ritual

3-D Archery

The Rattlesnake Roundup

Car Wash as Purification Ritual

Contemporary purification rituals, where water is the purifying medium, abound in the third millennium, just as they did thousands of years ago. We have the Jewish mikveh, a complete immersion in water to restore the observant to a state of virtue and piety; the Islamic ablution ritual of Wudu, where the hands, feet, head, mouth, and nostrils are washed in preparation for prayer or for handling the Quran; the Christian baptism tradition, and secular rituals including immersion in freezing water in winter, spring break at the beach, and hot tub parties. But nothing rivals the automated car wash purification ritual in efficacy, in systematized removal of dirt and filth, and in outcome. As the driver of the car, we experience the ritual minus the physical and emotional discomforts that can accompany a traditional purification ritual, and we reap the benefits sans the threat of annihilation. Enwombed in the safety of the cab of the car, we witness the utter transformation of our vehicle from unclean to clean within a matter of moments and experience this cleansing by proxy.

As in Dante's *Divine Comedy*, a Virgil-surrogate guides us onto the eternally rolling track where, once our tires are locked, there is no escape and no turning back. Suggesting the rite of baptism, car wash nozzles spray a fine mist that covers our vehicle, replicating the sound of a gentle summer rain. Next, an opaque, fluffy stratum of multicolored soap silently blankets the car, surrounding it in a cloud layer that vaguely suggests a heavenly abode and that insulates the driver completely from her surrounds. Momentarily one feels free of gravity, an angel-spirit floating in a rainbow multiverse. The cares of the world have melted away, and absolution is within one's grasp. But just as abruptly, this comforting layer is whisked away and we are back in Dante's Inferno. From all directions, the car is subjected to a physical violence to its body in the form of whirling, rotating strips of thick red chamois—the flails of Lucifer—making horrifying slapping noises on all surfaces as if they wished to strip the car not only of its filth but also the outer painted surface and the metal skin itself. This is the supreme test of the driver's ability to maintain the serenity induced by the previous two stations, and it is advisable to engage in a short penitential prayer or contemplate a future act of contrition at this point in the purification ceremony.

Although the lowest circle of hell has been reached, the faint light of Purgatorio—the second kingdom "wherein the human spirit doth purge itself"[1]—can be glimpsed in the distance. But first one must pass through a curtain of the purest water, which in some car washes is lit by a cycling color sequence created by high-intensity LEDs, not only suggestive of the tortures of the nine circles of hell now left behind, but also a symbol of the rainbow, God's covenant that "the waters shall no more become a flood to destroy all flesh."[2] Thus, the illuminated curtain of water can be understood as a symbol of the synthesis of heaven and Earth. Emerging from this station, one passes beneath the winds of Aeolus, and most, but not all, vestiges of grime and water are swept away. The shades of the upper circle of hell, consigned to an eternity of wiping and buffing, conclude the purification ceremony with a quick rub-down of the entire vehicle and wave you on your way. Paradiso is, by now, clearly on the horizon.

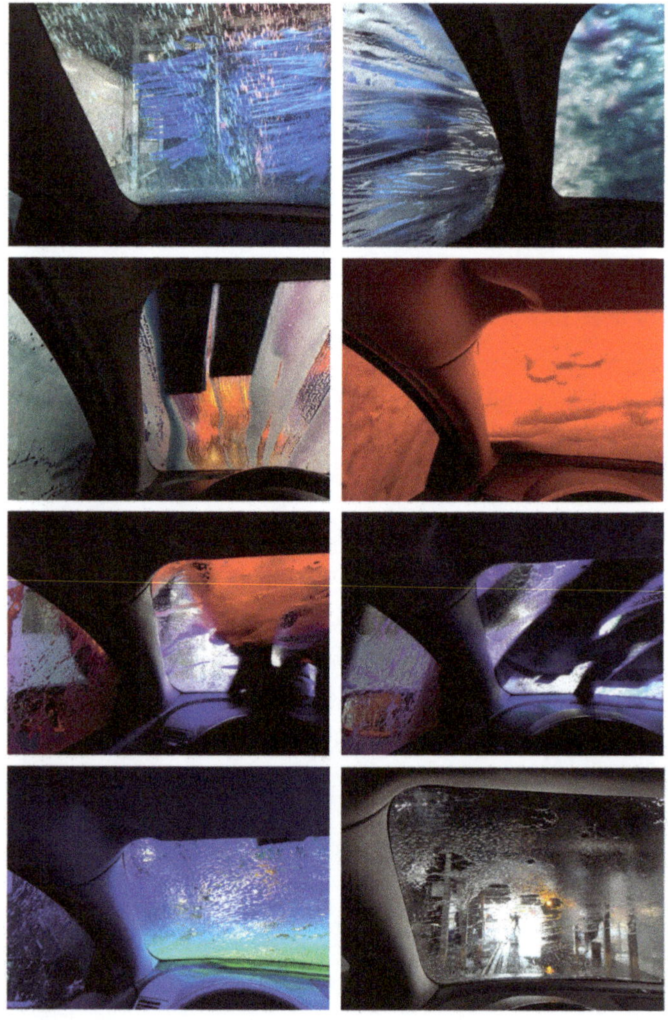

3-D Archery

So-called 3-D archery is a popular sport among hunters wishing to hone their skills in preparation for the dispatching of live animals. The 3-D archery course is strewn with life-sized, self-healing foam models of common game animals, such as deer, elk, boar, and rabbits. Adding an element of fantasy to the game hunter's experience, other not-so-common targets include velociraptors, cobras, carp, alligators, baboons, jackalopes, and even zombies. During the first two decades of the third millennium, 3-D archery courses have proliferated worldwide.

Hunting myths abound in every culture, and when contemporary man participates in 3-D archery, he connects to a tradition that is ageless, feral, the essence of traditionally masculine identity, and that stimulates the most profound depths of the primitive human brain. But there is also a mystery associated with archery that suggests the ineffable.

Ask an archer why he hunts 3-D foam animals, and he will answer, "Because they can't run away."

Even in today's secular societies, hunting is a sacred act that continues a long and venerated tradition having ancient origins and, as such, must be consecrated. As the bread and wine of Catholicism correlates to the body and blood of Christ, the self-healing foam 3-D practice animal becomes the animal itself, but not before it is sanctified by the high priest of the 3-D archery community. And who is this individual? In any group of archers, it is the shaman-like man who can grow the densest beard fastest, who most resembles a big game animal himself, and who drives the biggest pickup truck with the most deeply grooved, off-road-friendly tires. He can tolerate the greatest quantity of ritually ingested psychoactive agents, such as Budweiser, and his archery skills are enhanced when in the throes of hopps-induced perception anomalies. This man decorates his hunting bow with all manner of ornamentation, including special stabilizer weights, peep sights, vibration reduction dampers, and string silencers, and he proudly decorates his basement "man cave" with the skulls and carcasses of the animals he has killed, much like the ancient artists of Lascaux painted their cave walls with images of vanquished animals. The high priest archery shaman consecrates the practice animals by emulating the blessing ritual of the Catholic priest (also referencing the Hindu *puja* ceremony, where statues of gods and goddesses are bathed in milk and honey by Brahmin priests), but instead of holy water, the shaman sacrifices a can of Budweiser, popularly known as the King of Beers, and pours its contents over the inanimate creature, thus symbolically enlivening it and accessing its spiritual essence. As the Budweiser jingle tells us, "Where there's life, there's Bud," and conversely, then, "where there's Bud, there's life."

A full moon in October is known as the hunter's moon or blood moon because it was then that Native Americans hunted deer by the autumn moonlight, amassing food and animal skins for the cold winter ahead. In ancient Greece, one might have prevailed on certain gods and goddesses to assure a successful hunt and a comfortable winter, and Apollo—god of music, archery, healing, sun, light, and knowledge—was one of those gods. However, the most famous archer of mythology isn't a masculine god at all; it's Artemis, Apollo's twin sister, goddess of the hunt, the moon, forests and hills, and also of archery; mistress of animals. Artemis may be most famous, though, for her determination to maintain her virginity, and myths abound regarding the many thwarted attempts to relieve her of her "burden." First there was Actaeon, the great hunter whom Artemis turned into a stag for the transgression of attempting intercourse, excited by seeing her bathing naked in her sacred spring. Not recognizing their master in his stag form, his own dogs set upon him, tearing him to bits. Then there's

1.

2.

3.

4.

1. 3-D archery hunter and boar target.
2. Guiseppe Cesari, *Diana and Actaeon*, 1603.
3. 3-D archery hunters and zombie target.
4. 3-D archery hunters and mastodon mother and baby target.
note: 2-D archery targets used to protect identity.

Adonis, who boasted that he was a better hunter than Artemis, losing his life when a wild boar was sent by Artemis to contest the claim. In the interest of protecting his sister's maidenhood, Apollo tricked Artemis into killing Orion, Artemis's hunting companion and romantic interest. Given the dangers male gods faced at the hands of Artemis, these myths may, at some primal level, inform the reluctance of today's male 3-D archer to include women in this activity. An interesting question arises when one considers that Artemis was the mistress of animals: Is the act of 3-D archery, and the dispatching of flesh-and-blood animals that this practice leads to, the killing of the goddess herself?

The Rattlesnake Roundup

From Donald Trump and Judge Brett Kavanaugh to Bill O'Reilly and Harvey Weinstein, entitled, narcissistic, hyper-masculine, conservative white American men have never wielded so much power and authority as they have in the first two decades of the third millennium. This masculine power-grab penetrates all aspects of society, and throughout the American South, particularly in Texas, rattlesnake wranglers also embody these negative qualities. The rattlesnake roundup provides the backdrop for narratives of tyranny, misogyny, and the myth of the virile Wild West male, and these explicit connections, combined with masculine domination of a difficult environment, confer a deep significance on these events.

During weekend rattlesnake roundup events, usually held in March as the snakes are waking up from their winter brumation (the extreme slowing down of metabolism), thousands of rattlesnakes are hunted and captured. Men in paramilitary attire, who in everyday life are ranchers and business owners, transform into mythic heroes armed with snake hooks, trash cans, and gas canisters. They collectively storm local snake dens, spraying gas into their hiding places to force the hapless, torpid snakes into the open air. The captured snakes are deposited in holding bins, later to be milked, butchered, skinned, and eaten, and this elaborate ritual is conducted ostensibly to control the species. However, snakes play an important role in the predator/prey hierarchy, and when the snake population is decimated, the rodent population proliferates.

Rattlesnake roundups are distorted in another way. Snakes are considered a deadly threat to local communities; however, statistics show that people are more likely to die from contact with hot tap water, by accidental suffocation in bed, or by a lightning strike than from a snake bite.[1] Evidence abounds that roundups are more of a psychological than a physical purging, an overt expression of male rage.

Drawing on ancient Hebrew, Hindu, Egyptian, and Assyrian epics, rattlesnake roundups reveal that myth is alive and well in this contemporary, if somewhat bizarre, spring ritual. Customarily, spring represents renewal and regeneration, symbolized in the skin shed by the snake. But rattlesnake roundups are an abortion of spring: The snakes are delivered into the jaws of death while the redbuds begin to blossom and the oak trees unfurl their leaves. Most significant, some roundup participants point to the story of Adam and Eve as "historical" justification for their actions and engage in behaviors usually reserved for nations at war. Roundups are a ritual reinforcement of traditional roles and a murderous paradigm for the superstitious link between snakes, women, and evil.

The ancient Greeks understood the psychological power of snakes, perhaps due in part to the myth of Heracles. One of Heracles's twelve labors was to destroy the nine-headed Hydra (Hera, Zeus's wife, had trained the Hydra specifically to kill Heracles) and, additionally, the hundred-headed serpentine dragon Ladon. Heracles succeeded in dispatching both. Other serpent elements figure largely in Greek mythology; e.g., Python the Earth dragon, and, of course, Medusa, the snake-headed Gorgon. Informed by their tradition of myth, when going to battle at sea, the Greeks carried huge vessels filled with vipers and when close enough to enemy ships, catapulted the vessels into their ships. The vipers were a powerful distraction, if nothing else. Early settlers of the Western United States also understood the psychological power of snakes, hanging rattlesnake skins and carcasses on barbed wire fences surrounding their property to frighten and deter trespassers.

1. Newly crowned Miss Snake Charmer 2014, Sweetwater, Texas, Rattlesnake Roundup.
2. Frightened children viewing Western diamondback rattlesnakes through a window, Sweetwater, Texas, Rattlesnake Roundup.
3. In the background: Antonio del Pollaiolo, *Hercules and the Hydra*, circa 1475.

Perhaps it is more than snakes that roundups purport to control. Typically, roundups are men-only events, and women are allowed to participate only in ways dictated by men. These usually involve activities that reinforce traditional women's roles (the cooking of snakes) or that sanction the objectification of women, as in beauty contests where participants are no older than eighteen. Wanting to please their fathers, brothers, and other important male influences, the contestants all try earnestly to be the perfect woman. The winning girl often must milk a rattlesnake in front of an audience, inserting the young woman directly into the Garden of Eden myth and its snake/woman conflict. And, of course, the act of milking a snake by a girl at the cusp of womanhood is a ritualized initiation into her sexuality, overt in its signifiers. Worthy of note, in some roundups, the night before the activities are to begin, girls and women are not allowed into the areas where the snakes will be collected and killed, and if they appear, they are considered available for sexual exploitation. Like the snakes, the girls are stripped of their power.

Rattlesnake roundups connect to an earlier time in the Wild West when gender roles were explicit and inalienable, when fundamental Christianity was the dominant religion and people of different faiths were demonized, when animals were considered the property of humans, when outsiders were viewed with suspicion and hostility, and when crimes against women weren't considered punishable or even to be bothered with. Perpetuating these same damaging cycles in the third millennium suggests the Nietzschean eternal recurrence, a perpetual turning of the hourglass of existence,[2] and contributes to the many man-made threats to our very survival.

POWER SYMBOLS

The Eyebrow as Female Power Symbol

The Avatar

Keith Richards's Magic Stick

The Eyebrow as Female Power Symbol

With the invention of the motion picture camera, c. 1893, and its swift rise to prominence as an entertainment medium came the rethinking of the face as symbol and the role of the eyebrow as signifier. In this pre-Botox era, the eyebrows were an important conveyor of meaning and emotion. For stage actors, who were often lit unflatteringly from underneath, sometimes forming frightening shadows on the face, certain expressions relied heavily on the eyebrows when other features were flattened by this harsh lighting. Actors talked as much with their eyebrows as they did with their voices.

Actors in early films quickly realized that the stage makeup they were accustomed to wearing did not translate well to cinema. Early black-and-white films were orthochromatic, with sensitivity to all visible light except red, resulting in red lips looking black, skin looking gray and ghastly, and light blue eyes disappearing altogether. Eyebrows were heavily painted to compensate for this distortion of the other features: thick and dark for men; pencil-thin and arching for women. Think Charlie Chaplin and Groucho Marx; Theda Bara and Greta Garbo.

As film stocks improved over the decades and panchromatic black-and-white film replaced orthochromatic film, actors discovered they could be more subtle with their makeup. By the late 1920s, the thin, arched eyebrow was the established film look du jour, and women of that era sometimes shaved their eyebrows—then painted them back in—to exercise complete control over the shape, size, color, and arch of the brow. Since the arch is a symbol of the ability to support and carry an enormous amount of weight (the arch protects from collapse and disintegration), controlling the eyebrow was synonymous to controlling both the arch and the arc of one's life. Along with the Cupid's bow–shaped mouth, Cupid's bow–shaped eyebrows—curved up ever so slightly at the corners—created overt associations with the chubby prankster whose arrows fill the stricken with uncontrollable desire. Exaggerated and accentuated eyebrows on a woman's face signaled a desire to wed (or bed), unfortunately also communicating a modicum of desperation; and to stand under an arch, which symbolizes a future home, is to imagine one's own wedding. Clearly, the female eyebrow advertised sexual availability with the intent of attracting a mate, and the eyebrow has continued in its important role as communicator of desire and mystery.

Enter the eyebrow of the third millennium: a power statement of utmost potency. Women sport beautifully contoured, swept-back eyebrows mimicking the horns of an African impala buck or the graceful wings of a dove in flight, both statements of independence and strength. These eyebrows exceed the size of the normal eyebrow by some one-and-a-half times and wrap around the temples, like two slender fingers holding aloft a priceless Ming dynasty bowl. An homage to the Cupid's bow look of the '20s and '30s is still discernible, but the bow is flattened, more curved at the tips, and much fuller. These eyebrows are a signifier of the Greek goddess Artemis—huntress with bow and quiver—the goddess associated with fecundity; and the more prominent the eyebrow, the more the wearer signals her fertility. Large, voluptuous eyebrows are so sought after that some women with a dearth of eyebrow hair resort to a procedure known as microblading, where small diagonal cuts are made into the skin beneath the brows; these small cuts are then filled with a pigment and allowed to heal.

What about the unibrow? In the third millennium, the unibrow is the *ultimate* female power symbol. The unibrow is the utter collapse of the arch; it signifies a woman alone by choice, self-sufficient, seeking no one's companionship but her own. To pluck the hairs overlaying the procerus muscle (the muscle in which frown lines appear), thus breaching unity and creating two out of one, is a symbol of resignation, futility, hopelessness, and loss of power.

In fourth millennium BCE Mesopotamia, in the region known as the Fertile Crescent, the Sumerians developed their system of written communication called cuneiform. Using a wedge-shaped stylus (the Latin word *cuneus* means "wedge"), these early authors created lines of pictographs by pressing the stylus into soft clay. Proto-cuneiform's wedge-shaped style of writing drew its inspiration, interestingly, from the eyebrow, that most expressive of human features, and was in use for over three millennia, replaced in the second century CE with alphabetic writing. The connection to the eyebrow was thus lost, but the eyebrow's innate, symbolic power endures in the third millennium and beyond.

The Avatar

Originally a Hindu concept, an avatar is a manifestation of a deity that, in times of instability, can realize his material self on Earth as a derivative of the god essence. Vishnu explains the role of the avatar in the Hindu holy book, the *Bhagavad Gita*:

> Whenever righteousness wanes and unrighteousness increases, I send myself forth.
> For the protection of the good and for the destruction of evil,
> and for the establishment of righteousness,
> I come into being age after age.[1]

Because Vishnu is associated with the preservation of the cosmos and everything contained within it, he is the god most closely associated with avatars. Whenever the balance between good and evil is upset, Vishnu appears in his avatar incarnation to fight evil and restore equilibrium.

The function of certain African and Native American tribal masks is also to control the forces of good and evil, so in those ways, they are linked in concept to the Hindu avatar. In a symbolic way, the wearer of the mask becomes the god, the force of nature, the animal, or the spirit and is imbued with the powers of those forces. Taking this idea a step further, the masks of the Iroquois Confederation of New York state are referred to as "false faces," and when the mask is not worn, it is considered a living being and treated as such. Donning a mask is leaving the ordinary world and entering the special world of Joseph Campbell's hero's journey, and removing the mask is a return to the mundane. Thus, the mask provides access to the mystical world of the shaman, the traveler between the spiritual and terrestrial worlds. The mask is the agent of transformation and shifting identity, and both the wearer and the onlooker are transformed by the experience.

The notion of avatar has been appropriated by a decidedly secular faction of the populace of the third millennium, and avatar characters appear in animated cartoons (one could argue that *all* cartoon characters are avatars), in films (the titular *Avatar*), and in video games and virtual reality. But these avatars serve a different god. They exist not for the purpose of vanquishing evil and restoring balance but to entertain by engaging in contests between *virtual* good and evil. Derivative in concept from the Hindu avatar but shifted in meaning, the contemporary avatar is a virtual, graphical representation of a person and is considered an alter ego. Unlike the Hindu avatar or the mask-wearing Iroquois, contemporary avatars do not wield special powers outside of the virtual world, nor are they particularly concerned with the question of good and evil. A human who assumes the identity of a video game avatar is motivated to accumulate scores higher than his competitors via the annihilation of the other, and the avatar is the means to this end.

This appropriation of the avatar can serve an important dual function: avatars both transmogrify and disguise the myriad flaws and imperfections that make us human. Constructing an avatar can be uncannily emboldening and empowering, enabling the participant to create, if desired, an entirely false persona: a mask that both conceals the true essence of the individual and exaggerates this constructed, false essence. As an avatar, you can be Olympian: muscle-bound, strikingly handsome, confident in voice and temperament, and otherwise generously endowed when you are none of these things in "real" life. Sometimes virtual avatar creation software is startlingly complex, with hundreds of options for features like nose size and eyebrow shape but, more commonly, avatars are overly simplified images created in free-use computer graphics programs, substituting any nuance of appearance with the lowest common denominator. Feature by feature, the avatar is built from a selection of

1. Ravi Varma, *Sri Shanmukha Subrahmanya Swami* (The Avatars of Vishnu).
2. Iroquois "laughing mouth" false face mask.
3. The author's avatar.

perhaps ten different head, nose, and eye shapes, a few mouth shapes, a dozen hairstyles, and a half-dozen shades of skin, and individuals commonly distribute these cartoon composites, called "memojis," across social media, via microblogging (short, frequent posts), and through other image-sharing platforms in place of actual photographs of themselves. Clearly, these individuals are responding to an urge to mask their true identities, but one can only speculate about the motivation.

Recent developments in 3-D avatar creation make possible the substitution of the complete person, enabling the manipulation of socially charged situations from the classroom to the boardroom to the bedroom. If a teacher wants to convey a consistently calm, confident mien to her students, even when she is angry, her 3-D avatar makes this possible. If an introverted student wants to appear extroverted, by adopting specific gestures and altering his voice, he can. On a virtual dating site, a man or woman can make themselves into whomever they want and even engage in virtual avatar sex. Who's to say there are human beings behind these avatars at all?

Keith Richards's Magic Stick

In the Rolling Stones's South American concert tour film, *Olé Olé Olé! A Trip Across Latin America* (2016), Keith Richards provides a behind-the-scenes look at his magic stick, explaining that ceremonial use of the stick before a concert precludes the occurrence of rain. Wrapped in colorful strips of cloth and strings of beads and measuring about three feet long, the stick is used by Richards in a highly ritualized pre-concert dance. If he didn't perform his stick ritual, Richards claims, "It would disappoint the crew... They rely upon this thing. And the weird thing is, it works." A downpour during a performance in Brazil proves him wrong, but no matter: Richards is connecting to a long and venerable tradition of sticks, staffs, scepters, and rods as objects of magic and authority.

In ancient Egyptian belief, the sky was supported by four pillars. Symbolizing sovereignty and dominion, scepters (pillars in miniature) were allowed to be carried only by gods, pharaohs, priests, or kings. The scepter was considered an amulet—literally, an object that protects a person from harm (a good luck charm)—but also was a symbol of sexual prowess and male fertility. Important cross-cultural signifiers, staffs could fight demons, sunder the Earth, open a passage between the living and the dead, expand consciousness, and empower the soul. But not in the absence of some esoteric help. These objects of power, and by extension, Keith Richards's magic stick, often have no intrinsic power of their own and are imbued with their unique magic when blessed by a priest or other holy initiate, by the materiality of the object itself, or by means of special powers passed down through a series of priestly ownership. An object in its owner's possession, and in use for decades, by virtue of its being held, incanted over, and used for specific ritualistic purposes, Keith Richards's ceremonial stick would also evolve into an object of special powers. One could say that his guitars are also magic sticks.

Throughout the ages, magic sticks and scepters have held a special relationship to the natural world. Perhaps the most famous staff-wielder, Merlin the Magician of Arthurian legend, used his staff—inscribed with the words "to hold life and death in your hands"—to kill his enemies. In Greek mythology, the goddess Circe, a master of sorcery and

Keith Richards's magic stick. Stills from the film
Olé Olé Olé! A Trip Across Latin America, 2016.

spagyria, transformed unwanted visitors to her island into animals with her magic staff. And, of course, a rod is the tool of the shepherd, used to guide his flock. Circling back to the water management motif, in Exodus 14:16 (King James Version), God commands Moses to "lift thou up thy rod, and stretch out thine hand over the sea, and divide it: and the children of Israel shall go on dry ground through the midst of the sea." Moses's rod also produces water from a rock.

In the third millennium, the staff inspired the selfie stick, a telescoping apparatus on which to attach a smartphone to take a self-portrait. The selfie is a term invented "down under," where slang words are often created by truncating a word and adding the diminutive "ie" ending; e.g.: "barbie" for barbecue, "mozzie" for mosquito, "sunnies" for sunglasses, and "footy" for Australian football. According to experts, the initial use of the word "selfie" appeared in this email:

> From: Hopey ® 13/09/2002 15:19:29
> Subject: re: Dissolvable stitches post id: 169902
> Um, drunk at a mates 21st, I tripped ofer and landed lip first (with front teeth coming a very close second) on a set of steps. I had a hole about 1cm long right through my bottom lip. And sorry about the focus, it was a selfie.[1]

Commercially available in 2006, and initially considered by some a useless invention, the selfie stick has evolved into a magic rod with a single, special purpose: to capture one's portrait at a place or event of interest, then to share the image, sometimes with total strangers, over social media platforms. The selfie stick is also known as the Rod of Narcissus. As in the myth, where Narcissus falls in love with his image reflected in a pool of water, cannot separate from his beloved, and wastes away, the selfie stick user spends such an inordinate amount of time self-photographing that some have languished from lack of sustenance. Selfie stick users are often so entranced with their own image that they are seen striking ridiculous poses, pursing lips, exposing cleavage, and even photographing their genitals. They have lost the purpose of their lives—and sometimes their lives in the literal sense—using the world as a backdrop for these various narcissistic behaviors. As of this writing, selfie stick-enabled self-portraits have caused over 250 deaths, and the leading cause is, interestingly, drowning (lists of selfie stick deaths are available on the internet). The selfie stick is considered so dangerous that its use is banned at all Disney theme parks, at most museums, in North Korea, and at many rock concerts.

While Keith Richards's magic stick is a signifier of status and supremacy, he would do well to have in his possession a *weather* stick made from a dried balsam fir twig. Balsam fir bends according to relative humidity, so if rain is imminent, the twig will absorb the humidity in the air and curl downward from the extra weight. When the weather is dry, the twig will bend upward. With this simple weather forecasting technology, perhaps attached to neck of his guitar, Richards could preempt the embarrassment of a future magic stick failure, continuing to delight crew and fans alike.

TECHNOLOGY

QR Codes

The Cloud as Sixth Ocean

Segway

Acoustic Weapons

QR Codes

QR (quick response) codes consist of tiny black squares arranged in a matrix grid on a white background, creating both horizontal and vertical data patterns that are interpreted by a scanning device. Once deciphered, you are an initiate into the Realm of the Code, which in the third millennium represents a seemingly infinite number of commercial sectors, from e-commerce to nail salons to purchasing tickets for travel and entertainment to the funeral industry. In most cases, once you've "broken" the code, you become the owner of an object to which the code is associated, such as free panty hose or Coach sneakers, or you become one of the privileged few allowed to attend a ritual group ceremony, like a movie, a battle of the airbands (the frenzied playing of imaginary instruments), an office paintball session, or the creation of a sculpture made solely of naked humans. The number of QR codes that can be generated is an inconceivably large number—some say a number that exceeds all the atoms in the universe—so the possibility of depleting the supply of QR codes is a matter of zero concern.

QR codes find their origin in the Herculaneum papyri, more than 1,800 carbonized scrolls discovered in eighteenth century Italy. Buried ninety feet underground under volcanic ash, the papyri were found lying on the library shelves of a luxurious villa in Herculaneum, a city inundated in CE 79 when the eruption of Mount Vesuvius created a pyroclastic surge, flowing at more than one hundred miles per hour and essentially flash-freezing many organic-based objects in its path. One of the very few surviving libraries from antiquity, the collection of Herculaneum papyri were thought to contain many lost works of the great Greek authors and playwrights who we venerate today, but unfortunately, when an attempt was made to unroll the first of the charred scrolls, it crumbled into tiny pieces. Paragraphs and sentences were reduced to barely discernible single letters, essentially becoming bits of code. In 1994, electro-optics experts attempted to read these bits of papyri via computer-enhanced multispectral imaging, allowing the extraction of information not available to the human eye. During the preparation of the imaging field, a technician drew a black square on a white piece of paper, penciled in a grid within the square, and placed one hundred pieces of charred papyri

1.

1. Fragment recovered from a Herculaneum scroll.
2. QR code template.
3. Finished QR code.

2. 3.

within the squares of the grid in order to keep track of the pieces and their original locations. However, it was discovered that the ancient scribes who created the papyri used carbon-based inks that the multispectral imaging system was unable to resolve. In spite of the failed experiment, a eureka moment arrived. The technician recognized a pattern in the black and white array, a matrix version of the bar code, and QR codes were born. This proto-QR code is actually readable with today's technology, and it happens to be the code for a Himalayan pink crystal salt lamp from Amazon.

As the Herculaneum papyri are of interest to contemporary scholars, QR codes will undoubtedly be of interest to the distant future's curious. The ubiquitous QR code not only appears on nearly every product we purchase anywhere online and in commercial establishments, but also they are affixed to headstones in graveyards in Japan and in certain Jewish cemeteries worldwide. And we all know that graveyards are the favorite playgrounds of archaeologists. Since QR code data patterns are a link to information that exists in some other form, like the trilingual inscriptions on the Rosetta Stone, QR codes will provide important information about our culture's spending habits, products we preferred, our entertainment preferences, and the identities of our dead to curious researchers of the future. That is, if ubiquitous third millennium plastic products have not deteriorated, their QR codes unreadable or burnt to a crisp by a catastrophic pyroclastic surge.

The Cloud as Sixth Ocean

The cloud, a.k.a. cloud computing, is a third millennium technology that stores information in remote data hosting centers as an alternative to, or as backup for, storing information on personal computers. The term "cloud" originates in engineering drawings where a symbol of a cloud represents the internet, and, over time, the word "cloud" became jargon for computing that happens on remove servers. By blending two metaphors—air as the infinite reach of the mind and water as clarity—the cloud signified intelligence and precision. The term stuck, but the cloud metaphor is flawed on a multitude of real, symbolic, and mythological levels. Clouds are actually models of instability: the *opposite* of what we want in an information storage system.

Clouds are among the most ephemeral phenomena in existence. We've all had the experience of looking at clouds and seeing a form we recognize in them, like the profile of a relative or a fantastic creature, only to have the moment vanish as soon as it arose. It's as if Aeolus, the divine keeper of the winds, suddenly blew on his morning coffee to cool it down and in the process, recast the illusion. In art and literature, clouds and weather are often used to express the objective correlative, the idea that nature symbolizes emotions (e.g., a cloudy, rainy day suggests a troubled state of mind) and, like emotions, clouds are fugitive. In everyday speech, clouds are symbols for "obscured" and "befuddled." We have sayings for cognitive impairments that reference this: "cloudy thinking;" he has his "head in the clouds;" to "cloud the issue." Literature is replete with clouded-vision oracles, typically witch archetypes who predict catastrophic future events.

As climatologists explain, clouds form as a result of a phenomenological interaction between the sun and Earth. The sun evaporates (vaporizes) water, and water vapor, which consists of billions of tiny droplets of water, creates cloud formations. This accretion and distribution of discrete packets of information also describes computer processes, operations, and products; e.g., the billions of pixels needed to create a photograph or the coding and decoding of information across a network. But with clouds, as the accumulations increase, the droplets merge, become heavy, and fall to Earth as rain: a watery data dump. Clouds become electrically active; storm systems can evolve into tornadoes and hurricanes, and widespread destruction may be the result. A ten day weather forecast is correct only fifty percent of the time. Is this the kind of reliability we want to associate with our data storage systems?

The great conceptualizers of the world's spiritual esoterica used cloud forms as insubstantial stand-ins signaling the presence of the divine. Moses received the Ten Commandments from a God speaking "out of the midst of the fire, of the cloud, and of the thick darkness,"[1]; a cloud pillar led the Jews out of Egypt; a cloud surrounded Mary at the moment of the Annunciation. Job appropriated the cloud as a simile for the ephemeral: "Terrors are turned upon me; they pursue my soul as the wind: and my welfare passeth away as a cloud."[2] Clouds also represent Buddha mind. Like transient thoughts and delusions, clouds come and go across the sky, yet the nature of the sky remains unchanged. In Hinduism, clouds befuddle intelligence and cause delusion, just as they appear to cover the sun and prevent light from reaching the Earth.

In Greek mythology, after a dinner guest lusted for Zeus's wife Hera, Zeus created a cloud in her image to test the guest's integrity (he failed). Double-dipping and double-crossing Zeus, archetype of the entitled male, enshrouds the mortal Io in a cloud in order to ravish her. The word "nubile," meaning "to cover or veil oneself for a bridegroom,"[3] derives from the Latin *nubes*, meaning "cloud." The Wandjina of Aboriginal Australia are cloud spirits that created both the landscape and people, sustaining both with the gift of rain, a signifier of abundant ejaculate and fecundity.

Thus, clouds are places of instability and volatility, shape-shifting and unreliable; obfuscating and befogging; secretive and generative. This perfect metaphor for impermanence is deficient; cringe-worthy, even. Perhaps early adaptors of the term "the cloud" recognized their mistake. Or perhaps they were relying on our understanding of object permanence, first described by Swiss psychologist Jean Piaget, and our acceptance of the notion that even though we are not in direct control of our data, someone or something else is. (Object permanence is the ability of human babies to understand that when an object or person is not within sight or within hearing distance, the object or person still exists.) So even though we can't see our data, because of our grasp of object permanence, learned in the first few months of life, we trust that it's there.

In early 2019, computer engineers proposed a new name for the cloud: the sixth ocean. According to the group advocating this change,

> The Earth's oceans may be our most vast, stable, predictable, and uniform resource. Regardless of surface

phenomena, like rogue waves, hurricanes, and other weather extremes at sea, processes exist below the surface to keep the oceans stable. This is how we want our customers to think of our off-site storage solution. Clouds are impermanent and always changing; oceans are stable and predictable.[4]

Clouds are impermanent and always changing; oceans are stable and predictable.

However, the notion of the permanency of anything is ultimately absurd. When mailing a package at the post office, the question the mailer is asked is without logic: "Does this parcel contain anything fragile, liquid, potentially hazardous, or perishable?" Yes, of course it does. But if you admitted this, you'd have to avail yourself of some other means of parcel delivery. The Buddhists have expounded impermanence for thousands of years, and, logically, we know they're right. Life is a mutable cloud which is always and never the same.[5]

Segway

The name "Segway", pronounced "SEGG-way" begs the question: What is this device segueing from and to? The Segway invites comparison with the large-wheeled, horse-drawn chariots favored by the Assyrians for their royal lion hunts. The Segway, also having two large wheels, each powered by a two horsepower electrical motor, is similarly related to its tandem cousins, the kick scooter and the motorcycle, and vaguely suggests the motorized wheel chair. But as modes of transportation, the Segway and its handlebar-less knockoff, the hoverboard, are decidedly unsafe and uncool. Segway technologies require hours of practice to master, and riders are cautioned to wear a wardrobe of protective gear to prevent serious injury. Most Segways cannot easily negotiate inclines steeper than ten degrees, and for an accident-free ride, hoverboards must be used on the flattest and smoothest of surfaces, preferably the Zhangjiajie Glass Bridge in the Hunan province of China.

But what's ultimately uncool about the Segway and its knockoffs is not the products themselves or the fact that you need to wear a bulky, unaesthetic helmet for protection against an inevitable fall. It's the uncanny stillness of your body position while riding that's disturbing in the extreme. Minimal physical exertion is involved in maneuvering the Segway: a slight leaning forward or backward or to the left or right initiates motion in those directions. Too much of a lean to the front throws you head-first into the sidewalk, and too much of a lean backwards lands you flat on your back, creating the very real possibility of the Segway turning and running you over. Otherwise, the body maintains a posture stiff and wide-stanced, giving the impression that it's preparing for a great physical feat or exertion, as if the rider were standing at the edge of a cliff, girding his mental loins for the bungee-jump into the gorge below. What gives the Segway's predecessors their appeal is that when riding a scooter, a skateboard, or a motorcycle, in order to maneuver, the body is engaged with the device and must move quite beautifully and skillfully—sometimes with the grace of a dancer—creating the illusion that neither operator nor machine would be nearly as interesting independent of this collaboration. This is what's missing with the Segway. Because the rider's legs are eerily still, the arms not engaged for balance, and the gaze unwaveringly straight ahead, on-

1.

2.

3.

1. The Segway i2 SE Personal Transporter, Prague.
2. Young women on Segways, Washington, D.C.
3. Assyrian royal lion hunt, Okayama Orient Museum, Japan.

lookers confuse riders for automatons and understand them as persons only when they lose control of the Segway and end up on the ground, flailing on the way down. Indeed, successful operation of a Segway requires laser focus and an objectification of one's environment, mimicking a depersonalization disorder where the sufferer feels as if he's an emotionless robot disconnected from reality. Paradoxically, the Segway imparts a false sense of infallibility and power. One can only imagine the thrill and intoxication of the Assyrian royal lion hunt, conducted from its big-wheeled chariot, and though the Segway promises an equally exhilarating experience, the technology is at odds with its human operators.

Acoustic Weapons

For thousands of years, acoustic weapons have been employed to destroy property, to subjugate a foe, to elicit confessions, to cause physical injury, and to disperse crowds. When confronting an enemy, the ancient Aztecs wielded an insidious weapon they called the death whistle, a device in the shape of a small human skull that, when blown into, makes the sound of desperate screaming. One whistle is terrifying; one thousand suggests the zombie apocalypse. In the Bible, Joshua leads the Israeli army around the city of Jericho for six days, accompanied by seven priests blowing rams' horns, and on the seventh day "the wall fell down flat"[1] from the combined vibrations of the horns and the shouting of the soldiers. Ulysses orders his men—their ears plugged with beeswax—to lash him to the mast of his ship so he can resist the irresistible singing of the Sirens, whose song lures men to their doom. In 1989, U.S.

troops blasted heavy metal, Christmas songs, and random pop songs at the Vatican's Panama City embassy, intending to flush out opera-loving dictator Manuel Noriega. Today's long-range acoustic device (LRAD) emits an eardrum-destroying, brain-melting 162 decibels, the sound causing extreme pain and permanent hearing damage in people at a distance of up to one hundred meters (the approximate size of a football field) from the device. Intermodulation from ultrasonic sources, both intended and accidental, has caused traumatic brain injuries, depression, dizziness, and cognitive issues. And the infrasound device known as the sound canon exposes people to intense low frequency sound waves, below the low range of human hearing, causing an instantaneous evacuation of the bowels.

Acoustic situations that could be developed into acoustic weapons, or shall we say "persuaders," exist in our world with more regularity than we realize. Sounds that are merely annoying when short-lived or that are of relatively low intensity constitute the quotidian sound landscape worldwide. But take these sounds and manipulate them, and powerful and disturbing effects emerge. Human brains are hardwired to react, with a heightened aversion response, to the distress calls of babies, and broadcasts of their cries into high school classrooms could create a form of acoustic birth control. Capture the instant when a glass jar hits a tile floor, shattering into pieces, amplify and loop the sound, and

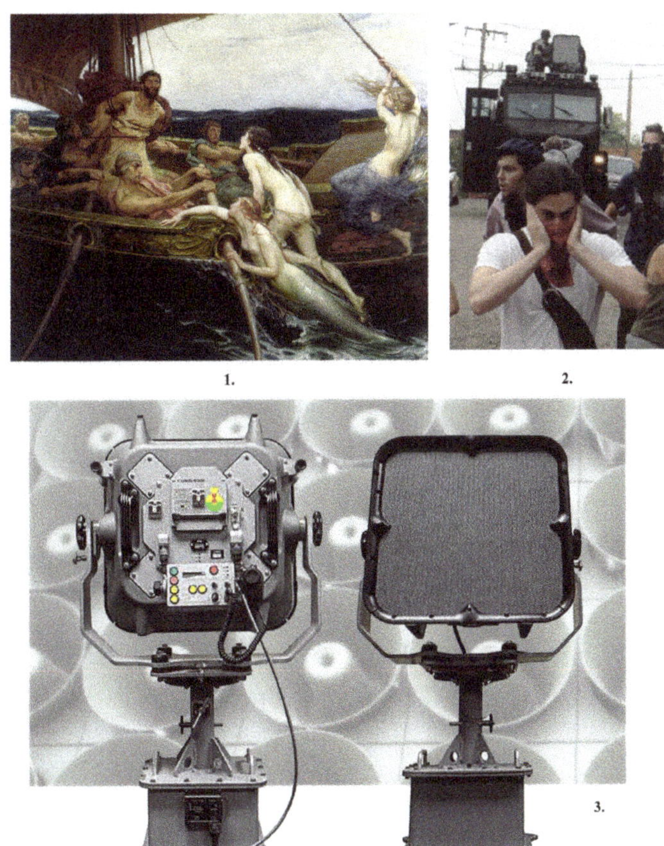

1. Herbert James Draper, *Ulysses and the Sirens*,1909.
2. G20 Summit protest (summit on financial markets and the world economy), LRAD acoustic weapon in use against protesters, Pittsburgh, Pennsylvania, USA, 2009.
3. The LRAD 500X long-range acoustic device.

you've got another effective crowd control device. Record the incessant barking of the three-headed Cerberus next door and blast the sound, at 4 a.m., in the direction of the inconsiderate, slumbering neighbor who leaves the dog outside all day while you're trying to write, and you may effect a change in his behavior.

Other acoustic notables include the chirps from a failed battery in a carbon monoxide detector: relentless, sonic daggers that trigger a surge of stress hormones. The constant, low rumble of highway traffic, reminiscent of the vocalizations of ancient predators, interrupts the sleep cycles of humans sheltering in their cave-like quarters nearby and, during waking hours, induces low-grade anxiety. The potential for generating effective acoustic distress, and hence weapons, is without limit.

Acoustic distress can happen in the most innocuous of situations. In *Travel for STOICs: Empowering the Solo Traveler Who Is Obsessive, Introverted, and Compulsive*, the author, an unsuspecting traveler, writes:

> The bus arrived an hour and a half late, kicking up clouds of dust as it coasted to a stop on the side of the road. In an instant, the isolation and ennui of waiting surrendered to mob mentality, and it was contagious. Conventional behavioral norms collapsed and the communal limbic brain kicked in, triggered by the thought of being left behind. Another long wait for the next bus was not an option. We made a frenzied, desperate dash to the door as it opened....
>
> I was one of the last three people to board the bus, and I squeezed in right behind the driver. I was witness

to everything he did, which included many things not related to driving a bus safely. As he pulled into the road, his forearms lay on the large and nearly horizontal steering wheel while he sorted and counted the day's pink bus tickets and stuffed them into a small pouch. Frequently he wiped his forehead and eyes with a dirty cloth, sometimes covering his eyes for seconds at a time, playing chicken with the road. Next, he gave himself a manicure, tearing the nails off between his upper and lower incisors. His head bobbed and eyelids drooped, and the bus drifted to the wrong side of the yellow line.

A constant backdrop to these activities was a game he played with the bus's high-frequency, high-decibel alarm system. When the driver exceeded the fifty-nine-miles-per-hour speed limit, the alarm emitted a shrill, eardrum-rupturing blast, the kind that either makes you want to run away or curl up in a fetal position, and neither were an option. He tried keeping the speed as close to fifty-nine as much of the time as he could, and since a bus is neither a precision instrument nor a machine that responds to subtlety, the effect was nearly constant no-touch torture. Enjoying any thoughts of my own, other than wanting to disable the bus speaker system in the most destructive way possible, was futile. I understood how relentless, high-decibel sound could make someone want to confess military secrets they

> had no idea they knew. Anything to make it stop. It occurred to me that Mexican bus alarms could be an effective addition to the CIA's well-known torture playlist (Barney the Dinosaur's "I Love You" song, the Meow Mix jingle, and "These Boots Are Made for Walking"). I opened my mouth in a silent scream; I imagined blood trickling out of my ears[2].

The acoustic invisibility of frequencies beyond our capability of hearing—about 20 Hz on the low end to about 20,000 Hz on the high end—make third millennium acoustic weapons particularly insidious and destructive. While ear plugs and noise-cancelling headphones help attenuate sounds that exceed our 85-decibel tolerance, we are helpless otherwise.

FOOD

Pringles Potato Chips

Energy Drinks

Peanut Butter and Jelly

Pringles Potato Chips

Pringles potato chips are the secular communion wafer of the third millennium. The foundation of the Catholic Mass, Holy Communion is the ritual in which bread and wine are consecrated and shared by the congregation, connecting by means of symbol to Jesus Christ's agony and death on the cross. When a group of young men gather around a digital display to watch a sports event—a vicarious experience of "the thrill of victory and the agony of defeat"[1]—with Pringles and beer in hand, they are in essence reenacting the sacred rite of communion, thus creating stronger bonds within the group. Interestingly, the Pringle suggests the shape of a cornette, the starched white headpiece of a nun's habit curved upward to suggest wings; cf. a television show from the late 1960s called *The Flying Nun*. One of the world's largest insight groups, Opinion By Design, studies how brands engage with the modern consumer and in a recent survey showed that 85% of Pringles users are practicing Catholics.

The shape of a Pringle can actually be described mathematically: $z = \frac{y^2}{b^2} - \frac{x^2}{a^2}$. This is the equation for the hyperbolic paraboloid from a branch of mathematics called multivariable calculus. (A function is deemed multivariable if its input requires multiple numbers.) The visual appeal of the Pringle could be linked to this elegant shape, and scientists have noted that the hyperbolic paraboloid, in any form, will catalyze the salivation response, causing the observer to want to consume all HPs readily available, a condition called "hedonic hyperphagia," the act of eating purely for pleasure. This is the classical Pavlovian conditioned response, developed by exposure therapy to only a single can of Pringles, and proves that any rational thinking process is bypassed in the presence of said stimulus. There's a reason why Pringle's slogan is "Once you pop, you can't stop." [2]

But are Pringles really potato chips? Actually, the resemblance to the potato chip is purely visual. Pringles are composed of a wheat, rice, corn, and potato flakes slurry, combined and rolled into thin sheets, fried for a few moments, then pressed into molds to create their signature shape. After a blow-drying process, they are sprayed with powdered flavors and packaged in cardboard cylinders[3] that in themselves cause the Pavlovian salivation response. In the presence of such a highly engineered food product, and with

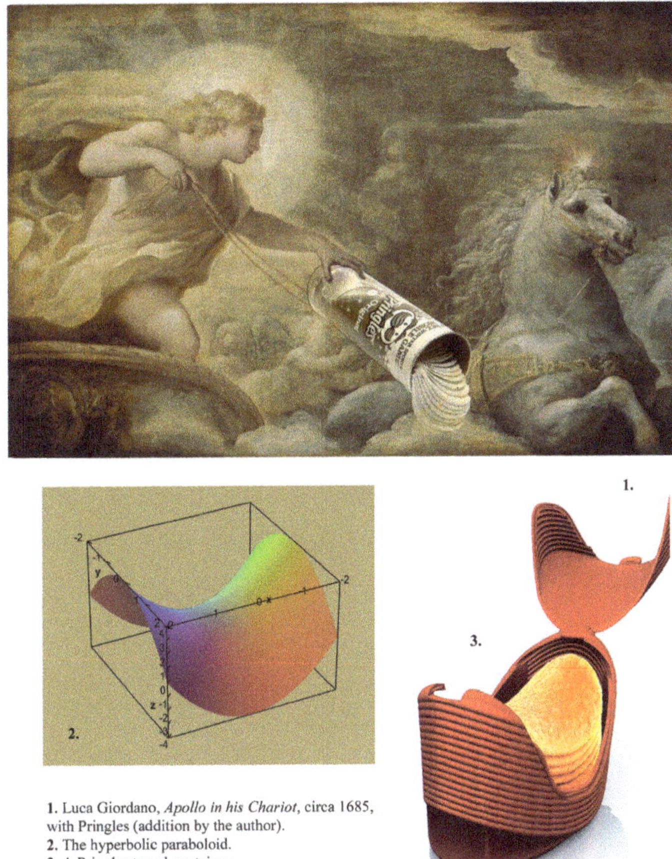

1. Luca Giordano, *Apollo in his Chariot*, circa 1685, with Pringles (addition by the author).
2. The hyperbolic paraboloid.
3. A Pringles travel container.

the promise of an imminent flood of dopamine on the immediate horizon, Pringles are irresistible.

Examining the Pringle from the neopagan point of view raises other interesting issues. The uniform, aerodynamic shape of the golden Pringle suggests autumn and the shedding of leaves that is the harbinger of winter. When nestled front to back in their cylindrical tin, Pringles suggest the long, silent sleep that is the activity of winter, but when opened, they are consumed with an earnestness that mimics the rapacious appetite of a bear waking from hibernation. The golden Pringle harkens back to the Greek god Apollo, the god of sun and light, truth and prophecy. One can just imagine Apollo showering sunbeams of Pringles down to Earth to be enjoyed by his disciples.

Pringles also suggest the microscopic world of the bloodstream, comprised of innumerable, uniformly shaped red blood cells busily floating through the body like little life rafts. One must be attentive and keep this image in mind in order to resist the temptation to eat more than just a few Pringles at a time. As Apollo was also the god of healing, he could bring deadly plagues if angered; if consumed in too great a quantity, Pringles bring obesity, clogged arteries, and death by heart failure.

Energy Drinks

Replete with symbols of ancient archetypes, energy drinks signify both the conferring of vitality and the quest for immortality. Found in the mythic traditions of nearly all cultures, the search for the elixir of life, the ambrosia of the gods, or the immortalizing soma of Vedic mythology was a worthy quest of these traditions' most revered heroes. With energy drinks, this tradition carries forward into the third millennium, a testament to its importance as archetype. Of great interest is the notion, common to elixir myths, that mere mortals are not allowed to consume any of these substances without suffering dire consequences. With names like Bacchus, Bawls, Cocaine, Liquid X, Monster, and Red Bull, the message is clear. Energy drinks are synonymous with masculine erotic power and with the "shadow aspect" of Jungian psychology, and not to drink them is to be impotent or, at best, ineffectual.

There are even drinks named Venom Energy, an obvious Biblical reference to the snake that tempted Eve in the Garden of Eden; Pussy, which is doubtful a feline reference; and Billy Boy, which features a smiling cartoon penis and testicles graphic on its can, its German slogan, *macht an!*, meaning "to turn on" or "to drive wild." The chemistry of all energy drinks is believed to be unhealthy at least and dangerous at worst, especially when mixed with alcohol, and this increases their allure among the American male youth demographic. Like the South American shaman and his ayahuasca-enabled journeying to alternate realities, to imbibe an energy drink with alcohol and survive the experience is an initiation into the sacred circle of god-mortals.

Prior to the appearance of the ancient elixirs in antiquity, it was written that the Greek gods fed themselves by sniffing the vapors of dead enemies. A few contemporary chemist-geniuses who have compounded energy drinks must have been well aware of this fact, given the vile odors released from some of these beverages. But vileness only adds to the mystique, making the consumer of the drink even more powerful—that is, if he both can keep it down and survive the experience.

When we examine the cans in which energy drinks are packaged, we see twin red bulls butting heads (cf. Taurus the Bull), the Eternal Flame, Zeus's lightning bolt, a mythic dragon, a snarling pit bull, the Greek letter omega (with its companion letter alpha symbolizes the birth/death cycle), and Billy Boy the cartoon penis. All are semiotically charged: some pledge eternal life, like the ambrosia of the Ancient Greek gods (as referenced); others promise an electrifying experience; others transformation into a powerful mythic creature; and all confer an increase in physical power expressed as masculine strength, stamina, prowess, and virility.

Peanut Butter and Jelly

Peanuts, a legume, develop their pods underground, and were first discovered and cultivated by the ancient Sumerians. Because of their scrotum-like structure and texture, and the fact that they usually contain two seeds, one per pod, they became a fertility symbol and were worshiped as such. A man who ate a handful of peanuts every day was assured of his virility well into old age. Another meaning assigned to the peanut came later and is associated with the Greek cult of Demeter. When Demeter's daughter, Persephone, was abducted by Hades and taken to his underground lair, Persephone was so terrified that she could not control her bowels. Peanuts were thought to be congealed bubbles of decomposing methane gas from Persephone's "night soil."

Toward the end of the second millennium, peanut butter, a creamy paste made of peanuts and hydrogenated oil,

Michelangelo Merisi da Caravaggio, *The adolescent Bacchus*,1598.
Peanut butter and jelly sandwich added by the author.

was invented. When introduced into the mouth, peanut butter sticks to the palate, and the action of the tongue rubbing against the palate to remove the peanut butter stimulates the release of feel-good hormones dopamine and serotonin. Hence, peanut butter grew to be one of the world's most popular foods. In the third millennium, the act of pouring a bag of peanuts into a carbonated beverage, followed by the ritual consumption of this potion, symbolizes the consummation of coitus and its assured success.

Jelly, a rendered form of (most often) the grape, is of course connected with Dionysus, the god of wine, debauchery, and fertility (and later a patron of the arts). Grape jelly is thus a symbol of his generative essence. A potent and intoxicating combination, peanut butter and jelly is a food consumed to assure fecundity, to honor the gods, and to participate by proxy in an ancient Greek bacchanal.

Acknowledgements

"Each friend represents a world in us, a world possibly not born until they arrive, and it is only by this meeting that a new world is born," wrote Anaïs Nin. This best describes what happened when, in an eighth grade English class, Susan Matthews befriended, nurtured and supported me: a vulnerable, anxious, and socially awkward thirteen year-old. As true now as it was then, she helps me negotiate life in ways no one else can. After each phone conversation or short-lived visit—she lives in Chicago and I live in Santa Fe—I feel a renewed sense of that world Susan birthed. A gifted artist, writer, counselor, teacher, and tireless humanitarian, Susan inspires admiration and respect among her wide circle of friends and colleagues. She embodies qualities that most of us can only aspire to. She is genuine, generous, loyal, reliable, compassionate, considerate, kind, and fun; plus, Susan is endowed with a peerless sense of humor. Her beautiful smile matches her equally beautiful spirit; the gift of her friendship is a priceless and irreplaceable treasure.

Geoffry Oshman, a friend of over twenty years, has been a source of support in numerous ways, an unwavering and compassionate friend, and a champion of my literary endeavors, for which I am humbled and grateful. When I feel creatively or motivationally deficient, Geoffry inspires confidence and ignites my desire to persevere. His independent spirit, uncommon world view, and exceptional musicality amaze and delight his friends.

Lt. Cmdr. Jo-Ann M. Joseph (1957-2018) was a participant in an Albuquerque, New Mexico, veterans clinic at which I volunteer as a sound therapist. Jo-Ann suffered with advanced breast cancer and, following the diagnosis, kept herself alive for twenty years by means of integrative therapies. To my surprise, she left me a small sum of money to support my work, and I am grateful to be able to honor her memory.

And a lifetime of gratitude to Dale, my first and forever mentor, whose last name I use for the password recovery question "who is your favorite teacher?"

Thanks as always to talented editor Kelsey Mitchener, punctuation and grammar expert extraordinaire.

NOTES

Introduction

1. Roland Barthes, “Myth Today,” *Mythologies* (Éditions du Seuil, 1957), page 112.

2. Joseph Campbell, “Prologue: The Monomyth,” *The Hero with a Thousand Faces* (New World Library, 2008) page 3, https://books.google.com/books?id=I1uFuXlvFgMC&pg=

3. Ibid.,page 1. https://books.google.com/books?id=I1uFuXlvFgMC&pg=

4. https://en.wikipedia.org/wiki/Archetype

The Roller Coaster Ride as Aristotelian Narrative

1. See “Acoustic Weapons,” page 117.

Indoor Skydiving and Dreams of Flying

1. The Daedalus myth references the Assyrian protective deity the lamassu (c. 700 BCE), a winged bull with a human head.

2. Sigmund Freud, “Symbolism in the Dream,” *A General Introduction to Psychoanalysis, Part Two: The Dream; X*. Vienna, 1920.

Guilting

1. https://www.whitehutchinson.com/blog/2013/12/americans-favorite-leisure-activities/

Lawn Ornaments

1. Ziggy Marley, https://genius.com/Ziggy-marley-changes-lyrics

The Wienermobile

1. Sigmund Freud, *The Interpretation of Dreams*, trans. Abraham Arden Brill (Nabu Press 2010), https://en.wikisource.org/wiki/The_Interpretation_of_Dreams/Chapter_5 [246].

Car Wash as Purification Ritual

1. https://en.wikisource.org/wiki/Divine_Comedy_(Longfellow_1867)/Volume_2/Canto_1
2. Genesis 9:15 (KJV).

The Rattlesnake Roundup

1. https://danger.mongabay.com/injury_death.htm
2. "The eternal hourglass of existence is turned upside down again and again, and you with it, speck of dust!" Frederick Nietzsche, "The Greatest Weight," *The Gay Science*, Aphorism 341.

The Avatar

1. *Bhagavad Gita*, 4.7-8.

Keith Richards's Magic Stick

1. https://www.visualthesaurus.com/cm/blogexcerpts/how-selfie-was-born-in-australia-and-took-over-the-world/

The Cloud as Sixth Ocean

1.

https://www.biblegateway.com/passage/?search=Deuteronomy+5%3A22&version=KJV

2. Job 30:15, King James Version.

3. https://www.lexico.com/en/definition/nubile

4. Suez Surric, et al., "The Cloud Is Not What You Think," *Computing Science Digest* (2019): 23.

5. Ralph Waldo Emerson wrote, "Nature is a mutable cloud which is always and never the same."

Acoustic Weapons

1. King James Bible, Joshua 6:20.

2. Eva Rome, *Travel for STOICs: Empowering the Solo Traveler Who Is Obsessive, Introverted, and Compulsive* (Santa Fe: Blue Morpho Press New Mexico, 2018): 78-79.

Pringles Potato Chips

1. Coined by Jim McKay of ABC's "Wild World of Sports," 1961.

2. To watch a Pringles promotional video, visit https://video.search.yahoo.com/yhs/search;_ylt=AwrUjdOT3AJdQSkADwAPxQt.;_ylu=X3oDMTB0NjZjZzZhBGNvbG8DZ3ExBHBvcwMxBHZ0aWQDBHNlYwNwaXZz?p=once+you+pop+you+can%27t+stop&type=8153&hspart=avg&hsimp=yhs-securebrowser¶m1=328bdddffcb442f193e1f8f3271e7a87¶m2=20190511¶m3=AVG+Secure+Browser%7C74.0.791.133¶m4=11%7CUS%7C1.17.4.396%7C1.17.4.396&ei=UTF-

8&fr=yhs-avg-securebrowser#id=20&vid=11bbef780b97311bdbe9b127a1d55e1e&action=view

3. To watch a video of the making of stackable chips, visit https://www.youtube.com/watch?v=tGt2wsS4tAo

IMAGES

My Visit to La Brea
https://commons.wikimedia.org/wiki/File:Heartbreaking_Tableau_of_an_Ancient_Mammoth_Family_at_the_La_Brea_Tar_Pits_in_Los_Angeles,_California.jpg
Licensed under the Creative Commons Attribution-Share Alike 4.0 International license. Author: MichaelEBM
http://figgis.agency/login/?u=lana, no copyright listed and no known restrictions on publication.

The Roller Coaster Ride as Aristotelian Narrative
"The Hero's Journey" adapted from Aristotle by Joseph Campbell. *The Hero's Journey: Joseph Campbell on His Life and Work*, (Harper & Row, May 1, 1990) the Monomyth. The Hero's Journey graphic © Laurie McDonald.
1. Revenge of the Mummy Ride, licensed from Dreamstime, https://www.dreamstime.com/editorial-photo-revenge-mummy-los-angeles-ca-usa-january-ride-enclosed-steel-roller-coaster-based-film-franchise-image75321216, © Ivan Dan.
2. Pre-opening advertising campaign for the Revenge of the Mummy The Ride at Universal Studios Hollywood theme park in Universal City, Los Angeles, June 2004.
https://www.google.com/search?q=revenge+of+the+mummy+ride&newwindow=1&safe=active&rlz=1C1GGRV_enUS751US751&source=lnms&tbm=isch&sa=X&ved=0ahUKEwjow_yzi9HhAhUC

HqwKHQYWASsQ_AUIDygC&biw=1242&bih=568#imgdii=sd HuOBMgrk7jhM:&imgrc=a1YuY6CSckSW4M:

3. Screaming mummy head, licensed from Dreamstime, https://www.dreamstime.com/royalty-free-stock-photo-screaming-mummy-black-image21308185, © Neil Lockhart.

Indoor Skydiving and Dreams of Flying

1. Bodyflyer at a FlyStation facility, St. Petersburg, Russia, https://commons.wikimedia.org/wiki/File:Sky-Sloth.jpg author: Юхапер.

2. Draper, Herbert James. *The Lament for Icarus,* 1898, https://commons.wikimedia.org/w/index.php?curid=13420511, photo: Tate, London.

Guilting

fish: https://emojipedia.org/fish/

text bubble:

https://www.google.com/search?newwindow=1&safe=active&rlz=1C1GGRV_enUS751US751&biw=1242&bih=568&tbm=isch&sa=1&ei=9QFTXZCWEtustQaa8bW4Dg&q=iphone+text+bubble&oq=iphone+te&gs_l=img.1.2.0i67l3j0j0i67l2j0j0i67j0l2.30659.32269..34073...0.0..0.106.868.6j3......0....1..gws-wiz-img.......35i39.Rz6cNLhknUo#imgrc=0KP_V5dT-yFChM:

Angry emoji:

https://commons.wikimedia.org/wiki/Emoji/Table#/media/File:Noto_Emoji_Pie_1f92c.svg, Apache License 2.0.

The Eyelash Curler as Architecture
https://commons.wikimedia.org/w/index.php?curid=27876445, author: Dega180.
Photo of eyelash curler © Laurie McDonald.

Lawn Ornaments
1.Metal lawn ornament musical frogs.
2. exhibitionist garden gnome: https://commons.wikimedia.org/wiki/File:Gartenzwerg_(01)_2006-07-20.jpg, author: Norbert Kaiser.
3. "Bathtub Madonna," Somerville, MA, © Peter Galeno, used by permission.

The Wienermobile
https://commons.wikimedia.org/wiki/File:1953_Oscar_Meyer_Wienermobile_-_The_Henry_Ford_-_Engines_Exposed_Exhibit_2-22-2016_(2)_(31777304390).jpg, author: Joe Ross
https://commons.wikimedia.org/wiki/File:Minimobile3_(2621303268).jpg, author: Jeremy Noble

Chariots of the Gods and Vanity License Plates
https://www.google.com/search?q=mitsubishi+eclipse&safe=active&tbm=isch&tbs=rimg:CeRXfhBA9Nv-Ijj5-u3xeDryZ7Oqvoe76yVNUbY5c9oDyKyjkq05KCxxUYkcoZQDjvykCLjEwNLzX8yY-k3zGZ79mioSCfn67fF4OvJnERh4MHqyO-XCKhIJs6q-h7vrJU0Re1d_1e9ktu3cqEglRtjlz2gPIrBGLi22ZiVXVMioSCaOS

rTkoLHFREXYQaEFr5vu7KhIJiRyhlAOO_1KQR0sGaEYBDtS wqEgkIuMTA0vNfzBET-qOX4susACoSCZj6TfMZnv2aER23e30sjeLM&tbo=u&sa=X&ved=2ahUKEwi8mKjR9cDhAhXBx4MKHbBXBpMQ9C96BAgBEBs&biw=1242&bih=568&dpr=1.1#imgrc=mPpN8xme_ZowDM:

Fidget Spinners

1.
https://upload.wikimedia.org/wikipedia/commons/f/fe/FidgetSpinner.jpg, credit: Florian Schäffer.
Fidget spinner in action background,
https://commons.wikimedia.org/wiki/File:2017-05-20-Fidget_Spinner-1578.jpg, credit: Superbass.

2.
https://commons.wikimedia.org/wiki/Triskelion#/media/File:Wheeled-Triskelion-basic.svg

3. Crop circle,
https://commons.wikimedia.org/wiki/File:CropCircleSwirl.jpg, Thomas J. Sutter, Jr. author, October 24, 2016, England.

4. Buddhist Ganykil,
https://en.wikipedia.org/wiki/Talk%3AGankyil

5. Three Legs of Man, national symbol of the Isle of Man, U.K.,
https://commons.wikimedia.org/wiki/Triskelion#/media/File:Three_Legs_of_Man_-_Triskelion.jpg, author: MartyIOM, 30 July 30, 2009.

6. Church window triskel, authors: 1st Ec.Domnowall, 2nd User: Perhelion,

https://commons.wikimedia.org/wiki/File:Triskel_type_Tonkedeg.
.svg
The Eyebrow as Female Power Symbol
http://www.dailyluxury.it/crazy4eyebrows-e-mascara-vamp-
definition/

The Avatar
1. Raja Ravi Varma, *Sri Shanmukha Subrahmanya Swami*,
https://commons.wikimedia.org/w/index.php?curid=13277149, C. Cunniah & Co. Glass Merchants 248-249 Devaraja Mudaly Street Madras (Ravi Varma Press, Karla Lonavla), Public Domain.
2. Iroquois mask:
https://commons.wikimedia.org/wiki/File:1890_Irokesische_Maske_anagoria.JPG, credit: Anagoria, GNU Free Documentation license.
3. The author's avatar, https://avatarmaker.com/

Keith Richards's Magic Stick
https://www.netflix.com/title/80148239

Car Wash as Surrogate Purification Ritual
Photos © Laurie McDonald.

3-D Archery
1. (Link not provided to protect the archer's identity.)
2. *Diane et Actéon*, by Giuseppe Cesari,
https://commons.wikimedia.org/wiki/File:Diane_et_Act%C3%A9

on_-_Cavalier_d%27Arpin_-_Q18573517.jpg, Cavalier d'Arpin, Q18573517, credit: Shonagon, Public Domain.
3. (Link not provided to protect the archers' identities.)
4. (Link not provided to protect the archers' identities.)

The Rattlesnake Roundup

1. *"Miss Snake Charmer," Hannah Smith, a cowboy snake-handler Terry "Hollywood" Armstrong, hoist a hefty specimen at the "World's Largest Rattlesnake Roundup" in Sweetwater, Texas*, by Carol M. Highsmith, https://commons.wikimedia.org/w/index.php?curid=51779409, no known restrictions on publication.
2. *Literally a pit of vipers at the "World's Largest Rattlesnake Roundup" in Sweetwater, Texas. Note the enchanted onlookers*, by Carol M. Highsmith,
https://commons.wikimedia.org/w/index.php?curid=51169605, no known restrictions on publication.
3. Antonio del Pollaiolo, *Hercules and the Hydra*, circa 1475, https://commons.wikimedia.org/wiki/File:Antonio_del_Pollaiolo_-_Ercole_e_l%27Idra_e_Ercole_e_Anteo_-_Google_Art_Project.jpg, Public Domain.

QR Codes

1.https://www.google.com/search?q=herculaneum+scrolls&safe=active&tbm=isch&tbs=rimg:CbafizQNyJnuIjiPJZ4dvwMY8dBkJZzildDEycpeZWau0k-nzsmv91xwBOddOF5CyyLCtmKAT_10e2-A0FpjyZYFtFioSCY8lnh2_1AxjxEUzO32ht3kD4KhIJ0GQlnOKV0MQRPWMX28xNOvAqEgnJyl5lZq7STxGvWfaJ9F_1pRioSC

afOya_13XHAEEXVTfoXLpDOAKhIJ5104XkLLIsIRPWMX28 xNOvAqEgm2YoBP_1R7b4BFcOmo4fNwvnSoSCTQWmPJlgW 0WEUzO32ht3kD4&tbo=u&sa=X&ved=2ahUKEwjZx9mY18Ph AhXM5YMKHWjVAPkQ9C96BAgBEBs&biw=1242&bih=524& dpr=1.1#imgrc=NKJ_H2lNMeESEM:

2. https://www.freepik.com/free-photos-vectors/qr-code

3.https://www.google.com/search?newwindow=1&safe=active&rlz =1C1GGRV_enUS751US751&q=qr+codes&tbm=isch&source=u niv&sa=X&ved=2ahUKEwjRpZ3P6snhAhUKKa0KHd8kAEIQiR 56BAgMEBM&biw=1242&bih=524#imgrc=pMAia2PIcumWiM:

The Cloud as Sixth Ocean

Licensed from iStock, https://www.istockphoto.com/photo/epic-super-cell-storm-cloud-gm947951224-258820061

Segway

1. *Prague*,

https://commons.wikimedia.org/wiki/File:Praha,_Ke_Hradu,_seg waye_-_panoramio.jpg, by Tomas Lollky, July 26, 2012, Creative Commons Attribution 3.0 Unported license.

2. *A group of people on Segways*,

https://commons.wikimedia.org/wiki/File:Crossing_the_street.JP G by Fourandsixty, March 28, 2015, Creative Commons Attribution Share Alike 4.0 International license.

3. Assyrian lion hunt,

https://commons.wikimedia.org/wiki/File:Lion_hunt_-_Okayama_Orient_Museum_-_DSC01748.JPG, Exhibit in the

Okayama Orient Museum (岡山市立オリエント美術館), 9-31 Tenjin-cho, Okayama City, Okayama, Japan, author: Daderot.

Acoustic Weapons

1. Herbert James Draper, *Ulysses and the Sirens*, circa 1909, https://commons.wikimedia.org/wiki/File:Draper_Herbert_James_Ulysses_and_the_Sirens.jpg
2. G20 Summit protest, https://www.google.com/search?q=G20+summit+protest+Lrad+acoustic+weapon&newwindow=1&safe=active&rlz=1C1GGRV_enUS751US751&source=lnms&tbm=isch&sa=X&ved=0ahUKEwjxl9LQ9JniAhUTj54KHQxlAsQQ_AUIDygC&biw=1242&bih=568#imgrc=DS6B9NUyfH4klM:
3.LRAD 500x, https://www.google.com/search?q=long+range+acoustic+device&safe=active&tbm=isch&tbs=rimg:CVbbfreKwZPsIjgxecpOlV_16kPBtzg4W4M2GI0XJUtkEzOEKP5fy-61smDn_1TFDf1Xga0JV9GefbapLUcKxWFwPqXSoSCTF5yk6VX_1qQEaACrx42K8-QKhIJ8G3ODhbgzYYRLh8ddcXi0X0qEgkjRclS2QTM4RHa8_1s8bsyiSCoSCQo_1l_1L7rWyYET0LQjk367w4KhIJOf9MUN_1VeBoRjy9ZUSEglwUqEgnQlX0Z59tqkhENiTQxHXci7CoSCdRwrFYXA-pdEYFsz1Hrjjxb&tbo=u&sa=X&ved=2ahUKEwiL-sr6x8nhAhUQoZ4KHQxTDekQ9C96BAgBEBs&biw=1242&bih=524&dpr=1.1#imgrc=Cj-X8vutbJgL-M:

Pringles Potato Chips

1. Luca Giordano, *Apollo in his Chariot*, circa 1685,
https://commons.wikimedia.org/wiki/File:Luca_Giordano_-_Apollo_in_his_Chariot_-_47.1566_-_Museum_of_Fine_Arts.jpg

Pringles can,
https://www.google.com/search?newwindow=1&safe=active&biw=1242&bih=524&tbm=isch&sa=1&ei=xAesXInNFqbijwTa65C4Dg&q=pringles&oq=pringles&gs_l=img.3...0.0..298649...0.0..0.0.0.......1......gws-wiz-img.1OJv_D-iC-A#imgrc=lCUg-yfWJ-215M:

2. Nykamp DQ, "Graph of a hyperbolic paraboloid." From *Math Insight*.
http://mathinsight.org/applet/graph_hyperbolic_paraboloid, Creative Commons Attribution-Noncommercial-ShareAlike 4.0 License.

3. Pringles travel container, https://www.sears.com/jokari-pringles-travel-lunch-single-serve-container/p-SPM12332658630

Energy Drinks

https://www.istockphoto.com/photo/energy-drinks-gm458709731-15957496, credit: skodonnell.

Billy Boy, https://www.test.de/Energy-Drinks-Riskanter-Koffein-Kick-4573293-4580833/detail/2013326!20/?origin=List&defaultprofile=suche

Peanut Butter and Jelly
Michelangelo Merisi da Caravaggio, *The adolescent Bacchus*, 1598, https://commons.wikimedia.org/wiki/Category:Dionysos#/media/File:Baco,_por_Caravaggio.jpg
Bacchus's right hand borrowed from https://commons.wikimedia.org/wiki/File:Portrait_of_a_Courtesan_by_Caravaggio.jpg
Peanut butter and jelly sandwich licensed from iStock, https://www.istockphoto.com/il/photo/peanut-butter-and-jelly-sandwich-gm454170501-26059106, credit: mphillips007.

note: All images public domain unless otherwise noted.

ABOUT THE AUTHOR

The semiological meanings of objects, events, art, advertising, film/TV, and culture have been a life-long interest of Laurie McDonald (writing as Eva Rome). In his book *When Do Fish Sleep?*, author Dave Feldman bestowed The Margaret Mead Field Research Award on Laurie for her work collecting and writing about single, discarded shoes found on America's highways. Laurie's film *The World's Largest: A Tape About Texas* is a survey of larger-than-life-size monuments—including a giant jackrabbit, peanut, and twin beer cans—built in small Texas towns post World War II. *The Sweetwater Rattlesnake Roundup* was a finalist in the U.S. Film and Video Festival, the precursor to Sundance. *Good Fortune Face* takes place during the 1997 reunification of Hong Kong and mainland China, and a face-reading fortune teller interprets Hong Kong's future in the lines, scars, moles, and discolorations on its new leader's face. And *Private Parts* investigates the fine line between art and pornography and the dangers of confusing the two. Laurie has received a National Endowment for the Arts Visual Artist Fellowship and four American Film Institute/NEA Fellowships, and her video art has been exhibited internationally at museums, galleries, festivals, and in academia.

In 2018, Laurie published the novel *Travel for STOICs: Empowering the Solo Traveler Who Is Obsessive, Introverted, and Compulsive*, a guide for successful travel with help from the ancient Stoics.

Laurie holds a masters degree in literature from the University of Houston and is a graduate of the Rhode Island School of Design. To learn more about her work, visit:

lauriemcdonald.net

bluemorphopress.net

whatittmeansthebook.com.

www.ingramcontent.com/pod-product-compliance
Lightning Source LLC
Chambersburg PA
CBHW061103100726
47911CB00012B/365

9780967899541